He knew if he didn't pay Harrison the money he owed, the man would kill him, so this seems like an easy way out...

Johnny rubbed his wrists against the back of the chair. The ties held, and his wrists turned slick. "I play the same table every week."

"And you lose every week."

Johnny grinned. "I'm about to find my winning streak."

Harrison took a step forward, but his hands remained at his sides. "You're always on the verge of a winning streak. Filling your head with lies doesn't lead to the truth."

"No," Johnny said, "but it makes me feel better."

"Do not test me."

One moment of silence bled into another. A bell chimed once and was silent again. The two male statues stood at attention.

Harrison adjusted his shirt collar before he undid the top button. "You really don't know what any of this is about, do you?"

Johnny shook his head. "No, but I have a feeling you're going to tell me."

Harrison turned his back to Johnny. When he turned around, he held a needle in his previously empty hand. Johnny's eyes flicked from the needle to the man and back again. The metal glimmered in the light, and a bit of liquid ejected from the tip.

The needle danced between Harrison's hands. "We have a race you need to fix."

Professional gambler, Johnny Chapman, plays the hand he's dealt, but when he's dealt a series of losers, he decides to up the ante with more money than he can afford to lose. Just when he thinks his life can't get any worse, it does. The loan shark he owes the money to demands that he pay up and sends his goons after him. The man offers Johnny one way out—fix a race by fatally injecting the dog most likely to win. A piece of cake, Johnny thinks, until he looks into the big brown eyes of the beautiful dog, and the price suddenly seems too great to pay. Now Johnny's on the run and the goons are closing in…

KUDOS for *The Fix*

In *The Fix* by Robert Downs, Johnny Chapman is a professional gambler down on his luck. He owes money to a loan shark and he can't pay. Rather than shoot Johnny or beat him up, the man offers him a choice. He can inject the favorite dog in a dog race, or else…But Johnny can't do it. The dog is too innocent, friendly, and beautiful. So Johnny makes a run for it. But how far can he go with no money and no luck? It's a cute story, filled with zany characters and some great humor. It also has some really tense moments. And it's short enough to read in one sitting, so you won't be up all night turning pages. ~ *Taylor Jones, The Review Team of Taylor Jones & Regan Murphy*

The Fix by Robert Downs is the story of a gambler out of money, time, and luck. Johnny Chapman is waiting for his big score. He knows it's coming soon, if he can just hold on a little while longer. But he owes big money he can't pay to a man with no patience for losers and drunks. He offers Johnny a way out. Fix a dog race and his debt is paid. But it's not as easy as it sounds. Johnny also has a soft heart and hurting dogs is not something he relishes. So he decides to run. But first he needs some money— and it all goes downhill from there. The novella is fun and clever, a lighthearted romp with a serious side. One minute you're laughing and then next you're biting your nails. Highly entertaining. ~ *Regan Murphy, The Review Team of Taylor Jones & Regan Murphy*

ACKNOWLEDGMENTS

If it wasn't for Gary Phillips, *The Fix* would have never seen the light of day. He helped me out when I needed a kind hand to steer me straight and, for that, I'll be forever grateful. Thank you to Black Opal Books for once again taking a chance on me and this novella. In the end, this is where it should have been all along. Lauri and Faith and the rest of the team have been fantastic, and I can't sing their praises loud enough. This novella is the best it can be because of you. After three books with y'all, I don't plan to slow down anytime soon.

I owe my dad a huge debt of gratitude. He has singlehandedly built me a steady stream of readers in Fairmont, and he's called in so many favors to help me out, I know he's lost count. My brother and his lovely wife, as well as my mom and dad, provided great feedback on my cover. My entire family who has endlessly promoted my writing and my Facebook page. My readers who ensure I don't spend all of my time talking to myself, and my fellow writers for providing tips, trade secrets, and countless rounds of encouragement. And I'd like to thank God, who always makes the impossible possible. Any errors in judgment have, and always will be, my own.

THE

FIX

A Novella

ROBERT DOWNS

A Black Opal Books Publication

GENRE: THRILLER/ADVENTURE

This is a work of fiction. Names, places, characters and incidents are either the product of the author's imagination or are used fictitiously, and any resemblance to any actual persons, living or dead, businesses, organizations, events or locales is entirely coincidental. All trademarks, service marks, registered trademarks, and registered service marks are the property of their respective owners and are used herein for identification purposes only. The publisher does not have any control over or assume any responsibility for author or third-party websites or their contents.

DEDICATION

For my dad and brother

CHAPTER 1

The taste of liquor still lingered on his lips. Six months without a drink, and he had the chip to prove it. His eyes were downcast, the table was green felt, and his wooden seat jammed the lower part of his back. The overhead light was dim, and he had his hat pulled down over his eyes. Johnny Chapman had lost three hands in a row, and he didn't want to lose a fourth.

The Indian sat across from him with his hands folded across his chest, wearing dark sunglasses in a dark room, his hair shaved close to his head, and a tooth missing near his front. He cracked his knuckles between hands and even once during. The sound bounced off the walls in the closet of a room.

"Well, what's it gonna be?" Thomas Kincaid asked. "I ain't got all night." His lips formed a sneer before he took a long pull on a dark drink. His eyes flicked in every direction except straight ahead.

"Don't rush me."

"If you move any slower, we'll both be looking up at the daisies," Thomas replied. He looked at his two cards for what must have been the third time.

Johnny sucked his lip between his teeth, flashed his eyes once toward the ceiling, and flipped a chip onto the deck. The roar in his ears nearly pulled him away from the hand, but the click of the ceiling fan managed to hold his attention. The darkness helped with his focus as well.

The girl sat across from him, dark hair drifting toward her shoulders and even a bit beyond. Teeth as white as a bowl of rice. A drop of moisture near her upper lip entered the equation. Her T-shirt bunched out at the front, and her eyes were as cold as Alaska. She played her cards close to her chest, and her bets were even. For the most part. She managed to toss in a few extra chips when she had a hand. But she was a straight shooter and hadn't bluffed once. Johnny knew it was coming, though. He just didn't know when. Even if he managed to run like hell, she'd probably still clip him at the ankles. Her chip stack sat more than a third higher than his own.

She had a good smile. That one. Not too much of the pearly whites, but just enough for a man to take notice. The words on her chest accentuated her assets. Tight, clean, and turquoise—the T-shirt, not her breasts.

Johnny's eyes flicked to his watch, and his phone buzzed in his pocket. The alarm. His leg vibrated for a second more, and then it stopped.

It was almost time. The medication. It took the edge off and stopped his mind from racing off to infinity and beyond. The man with the dark rims and the white lab coat prescribed it in a room bigger than the one he was in now. If he didn't take his meds in the next ten minutes, the headaches would start soon after.

The ceiling fan whirred again. The backroom was stale and damp, the casino out on the edge of the reservation with nothing but tumbleweed and small trees for over a mile. Diagonally opposite from the little shithole that he called home for the past several years. The rundown piece of trash with the broken Spanish shingles, cracked stucco, and clouded windows.

Seconds turned over, one after another, and, still, there was no movement from the Indian to his right. Lapu Sinquah flipped his sunglasses up, and dragged them back down, but not before his eyes looked around the table. The Indian made a face and flipped two chips onto the green felt.

The girl was next. She scratched her forehead. Her expression remained neutral. When Caroline Easton flipped her head, her hair remained out of her eyes. Her look resembled cold, hard steel. She followed the Indian with a two-chip flip.

Thomas tossed his cards away, and it was back to Johnny. He felt it: an all-consuming need to win this hand...and the next one...and the one after. Desire consumed him, after all. Or maybe it didn't.

The hand that got away. The hand that consumed him, pushed him over the edge, and had him calling out in the middle of the night. One voice. One concentrated effort before the moment passed him by. He couldn't imagine losing, ending up with nothing. Bankrupt.

This minute reasoning had him playing cards night after night, hand after hand, reading player after player. Moment after moment. Until the moments were sick and twisted and filled with jagged edges and punctured with pain. Or left him dead and buried on the side of the road in a ditch with half of his face missing.

The winning streak wouldn't last. It'd be gone again. Like a sound carried away by the breeze in the middle of a forgotten forest. This time, he wouldn't fold too soon. This time, he'd play it differently.

The one that got away. The pot in the middle that would have covered three month's rent. But he tossed his cards aside, even though he'd been staring at the winning hand for damn near three minutes.

His eyes flicked to each of the three players before he once more peeled his cards back from the table and slid the two spades to the side.

The Indian glared at him through the darkness and

his dark sunglasses. "Well?" Lapu asked. "What the fuck, man?"

Johnny tossed his shoulders up in the air. "I'm out."

"Just like that?" Caroline's long dark hair whipped around her head.

"Sure, why not?"

The Indian rubbed his shaved head. "You're one crazy motherfucker."

Johnny shrugged. "I never claimed to be sane."

The ceiling fan whirred faster, clicking every five seconds. The air was heavy and suffocating, and he yanked on his collar with his index finger. Two drinks were drunk, and a glass clinked against a tooth. One chair slid back, and another moved forward.

"There's over two grand in the pot," Lapu said.

Johnny gave a slight tilt of his head. "And I know when to walk away."

The Indian jerked to his feet and extended a finger away from his chest. "It was your raise that started this shitstorm."

"True," Johnny said. "And now I'm going to end it."

Caroline combed her hair with her fingers. "You haven't ended anything."

"I'd rather have that as my downfall than lose it all to you nitwits."

Caroline smirked. Her white teeth glinted against the light overhead. "Who made you queen of the land?"

"I'd like to think it sort of came upon me," Johnny said. "It sort of took me by surprise. Existence is futile."

The Indian smirked. His stained teeth were nearly the color of his skin. "Futility won't help you now."

The hand was between the girl and the Indian. Her assets versus his. One smirk versus another. The sunglasses were down, and both the movements and expressions were calculated. Chips were tossed, and the last card was flipped. Caroline took the pot, and her cold expression never wavered.

A ten-minute break ensued. Johnny used the bathroom, washed his hands, shoved two pills into his mouth, cupped his hands underneath the spout, sucked water from his palms, dunked his hands underneath the liquid once more, and splashed the water on his face. He grimaced at his own reflection, the dark, sunken eyes. He sucked in air and dried his hands. His shoes clicked on the broken tile on his way out the door.

His chips hadn't moved, and neither had the table. The stack of chips was smaller than when he started this game. As the losses mounted, his amount of breathing room decreased. His longest losing streak was thirteen hands in a row.

The blinds were doubled, and his mind numbed. Compassion was a long forgotten equation, and sympathy wasn't far behind.

The conversation picked up again, and the Indian

perfected a new glare. "I never heard so much chatting over a game of cards."

"It's not just a game," Thomas said. "Now, is it?" One dark drink was replaced with another, and the man's eyes glazed over.

The girl tapped her wrist with two fingers and flipped her hair. "I think we're already past the point of sanity."

"If there was ever a point, it was lost—"

"I had a few points of my own that were somehow hammered home." Johnny flipped three chips into the pot in one smooth motion. He had a hand, and he was determined to play it, even if he had to stare down the girl and the Indian at the same time.

"The game of life succeeds where you might have failed," Lapu said.

Thomas knocked back the remainder of yet another drink. "I don't accept failure."

Johnny's eyes flicked to his wrist. "You don't accept success either."

"Why do you keep looking at your watch?" Thomas asked. "Are you late for a date?"

The girl called and tossed three chips into the pot with only a slight hesitation. She had a hand, or she wanted to make it appear as such. Her lips moved less and less, and her eyes moved more and more. Her features were clearly defined.

Johnny kept his expression even.

"You're not late for anything that I've seen," Caroline said.

Both the Indian and Thomas folded.

"I'd like to take you out back and shoot you."

"Would that somehow solve the majority of your problems?" the Indian asked.

Johnny nodded. "It might solve a few."

"Or," she said, "then again, it might not."

The last card was flipped, and bets were tossed into the center of the pot. Johnny raised, and Caroline countered with a raise of her own. He called, flipped his cards over, and his straight lost to her flush. Half of his stack disappeared in one hand. He ground his teeth and chewed his bottom lip.

"I don't like you," Johnny said.

Her expression was colder than Anchorage. "You never liked me."

"There might have been mutual respect, but that ship sailed out into the great beyond and smacked an iceberg."

"Passion—"

"Does not equal acceptance," Johnny said.

"It will keep you up most nights," the Indian said.

Determined not to lose again, Johnny kept his eyes on the prize and his dwindling stack of chips. The girl to his right had never flashed a smile, and now her stack of chips was nearly three times the size of his own. His eyes flicked to his wrist once more, and he grimaced.

For several moments, the ceiling fan took up all the sound in the room.

His breath hiccupped in his chest, and he swayed in his chair. The wood jammed against his lower back, and the angry green felt kept an even expression. His mouth moved, but no sound escaped from between his lips.

He fell out of his chair and cracked his head on the carpet. For the next few minutes, he drifted in and out of consciousness.

೧೧೧೧

"Did his heart just stop?" Lapu asked.

Thomas leaned across the table. "What the hell are we talking about now?"

Lapu stood up. "I think that fucker passed out."

"Which fucker?" Caroline's chest pressed hard enough against her shirt to slow down her blood flow. Her eyes narrowed, but her hand was steady.

"The one that was losing."

"That's all you fuckers." She tapped her tongue against her upper lip. "You're all losing."

Lapu shoved his chair back. "I don't like losing."

"But you do it so well."

Thomas's body shifted in his chair. "Not on purpose."

The ceiling fan stopped, and the walls trapped all remnants of sound. One beat of silence was followed by another.

Lapu moved first. He slapped two fingers to Johnny's wrist and checked for a pulse. The heartbeat was low and weak and arrhythmic.

"What do we do now?" Caroline asked. "Have you got a plan?"

Thomas stood up and sat back down again.

"Cayenne pepper and apple cider vinegar," Lapu said. "Both have the potential to reduce the effects of arrhythmia."

She pointed. "Or maybe he has pills in his pocket."

Lapu nodded. "That is also an option. Check his pockets while I prop up his head."

"I need another drink," Thomas said. "I'd rather not be sober if a man is going to die."

Caroline rolled her eyes. "Don't be so melodramatic."

Lapu had watched his father die with a look on his face not that far from the one Johnny wore now: the lost eyes and the still body, with his spirit on the verge of leaving this world for the next. Lapu poked through his pockets in a methodical fashion and found a prescription bottle with a half-peeled label. He popped the top, poked his finger through the slot, and removed two pills. He peeled Johnny's lips apart, shoved the pills inside his mouth, and forced him to swallow. Minutes later, his life force had altered considerably, and color had returned to Johnny's cheeks.

Lapu nodded his head. "There's a purpose to everything."

Thomas leaned over and slapped Johnny on the cheek. "I believe in the possibilities of a situation. Those moments that lead from one into the next, filled with passion and compassion and equality, and some other shit."

Caroline smirked. "Which is what exactly?"

"Not losing another hand."

Johnny inched his way to a sitting position and slapped his forehead. "Fuck me—"

"Not likely," Caroline said. "It neither looks enjoyable nor promising, but that's a nice try, though."

"Your perspective has gotten skewed," Thomas replied.

"That's certainly possible," she said, "but I wouldn't be so sure."

∞∞∞

More hands were played, and more hands were lost. Johnny's stack of chips diminished faster until he was left with two red ones and half a drink. His even expression had vanished long ago, and his feet had started tapping during the last three hands. The Indian had six chips to

Johnny's two, and the rest were distributed between Thomas and Caroline, with the girl staring above a tower nearly level with her chin. Her expression hadn't changed, and neither had her methodical approach to playing cards.

The barrel of a gun dug into Johnny's lower backside after he expunged the last two chips he had to his name. He didn't have time to move or breathe, and he hadn't even noticed Thomas shift his weight and remove the pistol from somewhere on his person. But the digging did further enhance Johnny's focus and destroy his moral support. "Cuff him."

"What the fuck?" Johnny replied.

"It's time you realized the full extent of your loss."

Johnny couldn't see Caroline's expression, but her voice was filled with menace and hate and exhibited more force than a battering ram.

"Stand up, you piece of trash."

The gun shifted, and Johnny rose. The room spun, and he considered passing out all over again, but he pulled himself back and inched his way toward the metal door that was a lifetime away.

The barrel against his back never moved or wavered.

⌘⌘⌘

She hated cards. Had hated the act and aggression of

gambling most of her life. The thrill of winning and the
heartbreak of defeat neither moved nor motivated her.
Tossing chips into a pot, calculating the odds in her head,
reading players around the table, and playing the hands of
the other players instead of playing her own made her
head throb from the weight of the proposition. But she
did it, over and over again. If she thought about it long
enough and hard enough, Caroline might have called herself a professional gambler, but that was a term she hated
even more than the act of taking money from unsuspect-
ing souls who had a penchant for losing. But if her two
choices were paying the rent, or living on the street, she
would choose rent every time and worry about the consequences later.

She couldn't change her fate, or her odds. All she
could do was play the hand she was dealt, match it up
against what the other guys and gals had around the table,
and study the ticks and idiosyncrasies that made each
player unique. Over-confidence and euphoria were con-
cepts she knew well, and she could smell it coming like a
New Mexican thunderstorm. Even though she understood
what she needed to do, she hated her hands even more
than she hated long division. With each passing second,
her trepidation grew, and the calm she exuded on the surface was a thunderstorm underneath the shallow exterior.
It had gotten to the point that it was totally out of control,
and probably would be for the rest of her life. It wasn't

satisfying, or even mesmerizing, and yet here she was week after week, going through the motions. The same types of players sat around the table with the same types of expressions painted on their uneven faces. The voice in her mind echoed in time, and she did her best to keep the whispers at bay. But the plan backfired, just as all good plans did that were built on a foundation of lies.

"What the fuck do you think you're doing?" Caroline asked.

"Trying to win," Johnny said. "What does it look like I'm doing?"

"Losing," she said. "And not even admirably. You really are one stupid bastard."

She had been called to test him, to see if he would break and crumble beneath the weight of a bad hand or two or ten, and he had folded faster than a crumpled handbag smashed against a mugger's face. She had chipped away steadily at his chips, until two red ones were all he had left, and a tower of multicolored circles stood in front of her.

ᘓᕲᘓᕲ

Johnny had a hand that was planted in his lap by the gods, or maybe it was Julius Caesar himself. He couldn't remember the number of times he'd lost in a row. Six or maybe it was seven. The torment and punishment continued unabated, and he licked his lips more with each passing second. The hands played out one after another against him, and the gates of Hell had opened before him. The girl to his right was methodical, and the jabs kept on coming, one right after another.

Her hands were probably her best feature. The way her fingers slid across the table, shoving chips and poking at her cards, and prodding the weaknesses of those around her, only made him long for her even more.

But this was it. His moment. And he wasn't about to let it pass him by. Two minutes later, though, the moment passed, his chips were gone, a gun was shoved against his backside, and he was escorted out of the building.

CHAPTER 2

Gwendoline Pearce hated her life. Every fucking minute of it. It was one cliché after another. Her husband was fucking the lifeguard—the blonde bimbo with the massive tits, pert lips, and perfect ass. Tits that would sag to her hips in her old age, but at the moment were perky and flawless and exceptionally large. Her dyed blonde hair cascaded around her shoulders, and she had a dimple on her left side every time she smiled. Gwendoline could see the roots every now and then, and it made her want to hurl. False eyelashes jutted from the blonde's face, and she probably gave blowjobs that could last for ten minutes. Red lip gloss further accentuated the point.

Yep, Gwendoline hated her.

Because she had been her. Gwendoline had done the

very same thing when she was younger. She wanted a more sophisticated man with a pension fund and a comb-over, a workout fiend and a future projection of her storybook life with the white picket fence and the golden retriever. So she found and seduced one who had the next ten years of his life planned out to perfection. It wasn't difficult. The poor bastard had no idea it was even coming, and her toned behind led to a multitude of good times. It had been good and fun and might have been one of the best moments of her teenage years.

It was certainly better than high school. Walking those fucking halls every day. Being judged, leered at, and called a slut behind her back because she'd gone down on the pitcher underneath the bleachers during the homecoming dance, and thought no one was watching. Just another cliché in a life filled with bad dreams and bad decisions. It wasn't like she didn't have a few to choose from. But now she wanted to turn her life around, and she set her sights on a better path where the mistakes were just an experience from her past.

Gwendoline wanted success, but she'd been force-fed one rejection after another. If only one door had closed in her face, she would have reached an entirely different conclusion. But an entire neighborhood of doors had closed in her face with individuals of all ages and races, colors and creeds, and probably even religions as well slamming the pine from five to nine. If she had any tears left, she would have shed a few, and possibly a few more. It would have been scenic and oceanic and possibly even picturesque. But it beat her down: one wave after another crashing into her soul and sucking out the marrow from her bones. Her hand shook. She hadn't smoked a cigarette in three years, but she wanted one now. Craved the opportunity to suck that nicotine into her soul, have it commune with her body, and calm her nerves.

Her running had improved since she gave up the nicotine. Sure, initially it sucked like a mother when she tried to go even three hundred feet, but then she was able to go three hundred more. She'd pushed herself, shoved herself past the limit of intolerance, until it was all so tolerable. So hopeful and easy and comfortable. And that might have been it, except she had to keep going. To keep moving.

She had her dreams. But those had been sucked away from her by the pitcher underneath the bleachers. After all those doors closed, she didn't think she'd be able to keep going. But she put one foot in front of the other and moved. Even when it would have been easier to stand still. Now it wasn't even in the same vicinity.

The street was crammed with people, shoulder-to-shoulder, the sounds surrounding her overwhelming, one on top of the other.

The gaps in her head misfired, with the synapses far out of place, whispers filled the gaps and the spaces, and she looked around with a sense of abandon, the place unfamiliar to her.

Footsteps toppled one on top of the other, and she glanced over her right shoulder, then her left, and both times there was a sense of innocence in the women and children, and the men with the baby faces and the pinstriped business suits.

Gwendoline passed streetlamps and street signs and storefronts and a broken down car in a broken down alley. The same broken down car backfired, as the puff of exhaust mingled with the New Mexican afternoon. She'd passed four intersections and was well on her way toward a fifth when a hand reached out and snagged her shoulder.

Her head whipped around, her dark hair flipping about her face, her arms already locked in an offensive gesture. "What the hell do you think you're doing?"

"I need to talk to you."

The sunglasses were unnecessary on the unusually cloudy day, and his outfit was bright blue. His expression lacked all basic emotion. His frame was lanky, his hair was short, and his voice cut through the air faster than a switchblade. While he was unfamiliar to her, his presence was not.

She ground her teeth. "So talk."

"Not here," the man said. "Not now. We'll call you."

The separation between them increased slightly.

Strange faces and strange people pushed forward on either side of them. No one stopped to stare.

When a gap formed, her shoulders straightened. "You'll call me?"

"We have your number." His tone was methodical, even.

Her body sagged several inches. "Oh."

He took a half-step forward. "Your number is listed."

"I changed my last name."

"We have your new one."

Her body sagged another inch, and, in the distance, a woman screamed. Or it might have been the wind. "I'm sure you do." The silence stretched for several beats. "You're not going to cause me trouble, are you?"

He shrugged and disappeared into the next mass of bodies. A nondescript man in a rather distinct place where neon signs advertised long forgotten trends and previous fashions lined up like dominoes. Bars, restaurants, stores, and a flagship university intertwined on a single street in the heart of downtown with college kids patrolling the avenue.

Had they just killed her and put her out of her misery, fear wouldn't follow her around every bend in the road. If she had the nerve, she would have done it herself and left this place for a one-way ticket to the next. But the thought of dangling from a chandelier, or consuming a massive amount of pills, or slitting her wrists in the bathtub, just seemed a bit too cliché in a world already filled with too many of them. But the thought did cross her mind multiple times. Many of which occurred on days like today, when her mind overflowed with rot and decay.

Or she could have careened off a ravine. Ended her life in a bright blue muscle car, a Mustang, that made her feel special on some level, as she careened down the Sandia mountain pass and tossed herself toward the sand below. A ball of orange flame against an orange-colored sky. It was a simple solution to a much more complicated problem.

But she did give a damn.

❧❧❧

Fuck. He'd lost his entire stash to a woman. And it wasn't even his money to lose. Well, he'd borrowed it, because he knew he couldn't lose, like betting on the ponies in the middle of a Thursday afternoon. Certainty in an uncertain world. Desire built him up, along with need and simple solutions to more complicated problems, and he paraded around in a sea of despair. A wonderful life filled with darkness and gray. He sought adventure when the status quo would do. He couldn't move on. Instead, he clung to the past. At least that's what his last five girl-friends had said. Right before he told them to go fuck themselves. At least one of them probably would have. The one with the wild hair and the wild streak, and the string of ex-boyfriends banging on his front door at three o'clock in the morning.

The desk was long and thick and covered in masculine undertones. The overhead lights were turned off, and the glow of a single lamp offered a hint of light in the otherwise dark room.

A grandfather clock stood at attention in one corner, and three men in dark suits did the same in the other. Emptiness and despair took up residence in the large space.

For five minutes, Johnny Chapman sat and waited and stared over the top of the desk. One of the men coughed, and then all was silent once more.

Harrison Barrymore looked up from the stack of papers piled high on his desk, ran a hand through his gray hair, and flicked his chin at his Rolex watch. "What do you mean, you lost it?"

Johnny coughed into his right fist. "I thought I could win."

Harrison's presence shifted to the left. "You always think that. Every gambler I've ever known never walks into a situation and tells the world he's going to lose his shirt. But you—" A finger was extended. "—you somehow think you're different than all the rest. That somehow you're special."

Johnny closed his fist even tighter. "That makes me feel infinitely better."

Harrison wrote for several moments and then looked up. "I'm just trying to help out a friend."

Pressure built at the back of Johnny's head. "Maybe you should try a little harder."

A leg shifted, and a chair squeaked.

"I wouldn't want to get your hopes up too much."

The office was on the fourteenth floor, and double wooden doors stood at attention at the opposite end away from the desk. The walk had been arduous, and Johnny's hands were still cuffed behind his back. The leather felt cool against his palms, and when he shifted his position, his mind shifted and fractured along with the subtle movement.

The car ride had been more tortuous than the steps it had taken to get him to his present location. Two of the three men had sat on either side of him in the back. The one on his left side had tossed a series of elbows against his ribs, and Johnny had doubled over on two occasions, but he had somehow managed to keep his composure.

The silence was about as subtle as a submachine gun. A steady ringing in his ears caused him to shift his head.

Harrison walked around his desk and shoved a hand against Johnny's chest. The large man tilted Johnny's head in the direction of the open window.

"I don't see anything," Johnny said.

Harrison exhaled one breath followed by a second. "You never were that good at forward thinking."

"True."

Harrison took a step back. "Maybe you should move on."

The worst position possible was the one Johnny often found himself in the middle of. Difficult situations were often proved even worse when stupidity managed to get in the way. "If I could, I would."

Harrison returned to the other side of his desk and resumed his position in his brown leather chair. "More likely, you just won't."

Johnny narrowed his eyes and adjusted his hands. "That's certainly a possibility as well."

"Life is filled with them," Harrison said. "But somehow you manage to find all the wrong ones. You have a knack for drowning. One might even call it a death wish."

Johnny had been good once, before his life had gone to shit, and the debt had mounted up four figures at a time. Sometimes five. He had often reached an atypical result in what was a typical situation.

Johnny grinned for the first time that day. "I have a death plan."

Harrison clasped his hands together on top of his desk. "And does it involve some sort of crazy-assed, far-fetched scenario?"

Johnny said nothing.

"You do realize there's no way for you to win at this particular game. You're going to find yourself swallowing saltwater on a sandy shore not far from the Mexico coast. If that doesn't manage to kill you, I foresee a big explosion followed by a violent death, and your charcoaled remains shoved out to sea."

Johnny had never set foot on a beach let alone the water. "What the hell are you talking about?"

"A clue to your dramatic demise. Or a shred of hope instead of a moment of weakness. Makes no difference."

Johnny offered up one look and then another. "You're killing me."

"That wasn't the general idea. You see, I have plans for you."

∽∾∽

The bar was loud, and so was the crowd. Her third drink went down easier than the first two, and the bartender offered her up a smile, a wink, and a come-hither glance. Gwendoline declined. The alcohol dropped her inhibitions to a monotone level. The music pulsated around her, and the palms of her hands were wet. The spot on the bar where her glass sat was dirty and scarred, and the mirror just above her eye line was convex.

The gentleman to her right was no gentleman at all, and there was a white line around his left ring finger. His smile was bright, and his gestures were sweeping and grand. His eyes were sunken and hollow, and the bones on his face stuck out at unusual angles. His conversational skills were severely lacking, and his expression had reached a level of morose. He tapped his fingers on the bar to the beat of the music. She placed hers in her lap.

When gaps stepped across the conversational threshold, she turned her head away and focused on the empty seat next to her. He was more interested in himself than he was in her, and he said his name was Jim, or it might have been Tim. Either way, it didn't matter. His job didn't matter, and neither did he.

His smile was reptilian.

"You really are a bastard," Gwendoline said.

"Am I bothering you?"

"Your problems will come to the surface, and you'll have to face reality with your pants around your ankles."

His hair stuck out on top of his head at obscene angles, and he took small, measured sips from the glass in front of him. "Contrite?"

"It will be less dramatic this way. You might even make it out of this bar alive."

The dance floor was covered with a mass of bodies, and the exits were covered with men and women chatting away, a few of whom were sucking at each other's necks. Her escape options were limited, but then again, so were his. She didn't feel threatened, just claustrophobic.

He reached a hand out to touch her face, and she pulled her head away. "You really are a fucking bastard."

"The extent of my abilities is endless," he said. "We've barely scratched the surface."

"Just keep all of it in mind next time when you're staring down the barrel of a gun." She formed her right hand into a pistol and dropped her thumb on top of her index finger. "I don't miss."

His back stiffened, and his drink sloshed atop the wood. "I don't like guns."

"What business are you in, exactly?"

"Precious metals."

Gwendoline narrowed her eyes.

"I never did like my job," he said.

⁊∽⁊

The keys bounced in his hand. Johnny juggled them in his left while he balanced the cup of coffee with his right. The steps came quicker. Faster. The beat increased in his head, and his feet clambered to keep up. He sucked in his lip. His teeth clicked against each other, while his mind clicked and bounced and raced.

The car moved forward in traffic. His car. Not fast. Not slow. Keeping pace with the cars around it. He never sped, never had a ticket on his record. Not even parking. He was a lucky bastard. Or at least he thought he was, but now he wasn't so sure. His mind drifted along with his car. A horn honked. Distant. The light turned green, and he plowed ahead. His foot pressed against the floor, and the car jerked forward. The engine revved, and so did his mind, faster and faster until the images blurred, and the pain subsided.

The problems mounted up, one on top of another, until his mind drowned and filled with saltwater. The solutions didn't come easy, if at all. He played the hand in his mind over and over again. Harrison's words and actions played on, repeating like an image stuck in his rearview mirror. Johnny found himself careening, and his problems dangled over the edge of a cliff. He thought about the present and the past. But he had no idea about the future.

The sound of death surrounded him. Like a four-car accident on I-25 on the day after Thanksgiving. The losses piled up in his head and on his lap. And, still, he moved forward. He pressed his foot on the accelerator and continued to hope for the best.

Taillights entered his line of sight, but he had no thoughts of exiting. Music blared through speakers from the car to his right. A song he didn't recognize from a band that wasn't familiar. Modern rock, filled with bass and guitar and screeching vocals from a voice that could have just as easily been masculine or feminine.

His world ricocheted with more force than a wreck-

ing ball. His effervescent intuition kept him sane and focused on the task at hand. Or then again maybe it
wouldn't. Maybe it was counterintuitive. Or counterpro-
ductive.

His right cheek still stung from Harrison's slap and
harsh words. Johnny had one way out of his financial ca-
lamity, but it might as well have been no way at all.

The wind ground against his small car, clanging
against metal and howling. Or it could have been the
sound of his mind shutting down, unable to deal with this
unexpected situation.

CHAPTER 3

The punch landed on Johnny's jaw. He spun around, smacking the edge of the bar, before landing flat on his ass. The floor was hard against his back, and his eyes were pointed at the ceiling. The beauty of it was, he could still take a punch. The bad part of it was he was now on his ass looking up at a barrel of a man standing over him, the man scowling down with fierce determination and unused energy.

Johnny rolled away from him and trundled to his feet. Crawling might have been beneath him in another life, but this was a new one, and the new superseded the old, sitting on the edge of the precipice he had fallen over, as the alcohol lumbered its way through his system.

The first drink had gone down easier than the second. The third punch had hit harder than the first two and managed to catch him off guard. He stretched his chin and rubbed his jaw, and stared at a sea of patrons focused in his direction with mouths agape and jaws askew. The two drinks had calmed his nerves, and the third punch had placed him in a rather awkward situation. Harrison had neither helped with the awkwardness nor the situation, but he did have more than one prophetic conclusion spouted in Johnny's direction.

Johnny's car had led him to the bar, and he didn't have the willpower to turn away from the pouncing tide. His present situation led him to the drinking, and stubbornness had led him to the bar fight with the man who spewed arrogance the way fishermen spewed foul words. He was a younger version of Harrison, with nearly as much confidence and not as many years under his belt.

Johnny swung a hard right followed by a hard left. Neither punch smacked its intended destination, as another blow struck his left cheek.

"What the fuck do you think you're doing?" the man asked.

Johnny grunted in response.

"I asked you a question."

Johnny lifted his chin. "And I wish I had an answer for you."

The man moved to his right, and then his pile driver of an arm struck Johnny's chin once again. Prepared for it this time, Johnny stood his ground.

"Are you trying to be funny?"

Johnny shook his head. "No."

"If your trap opens again, I'll hit you so hard your grandchildren will feel the blow. You might want to keep that in mind the next time you go running your mouth."

"I didn't plan on having it run anywhere," Johnny said, "to be perfectly honest with you."

"And I don't like you," the man replied.

Johnny wiped a dab of blood off his lower lip. "You made that perfectly clear about six minutes ago."

"Five."

The man shoved his way through the crowd before Johnny could offer a pointed reply.

His ears hurt. The ringing had lasted five minutes, the extent of his present predicament, and he would have been forced to repeat himself a time or two, if he didn't want to get the fuck out of Albuquerque right now. Not tomorrow. Not today. Yesterday. If he hadn't been one fucked-up mess to begin with, he might have entered the bar with a different mindset.

The bar fight had seemed like an excellent idea at the time. A way to take his mind off his tragic bane of an existence. But he hadn't exactly picked the right guy, and he hadn't exactly picked the right time. And his cowboy reputation was flushed down the toilet and left at the bottom of a sewer. If he was being perfectly honest with himself, telling the truth was one giant pain in the ass.

And it was exactly how he ended up on his ass in the first place.

He hadn't even tied his shoes correctly this morning. He had skipped a loop and had poured coffee down the front of his shirt. The fucking passenger seat was a pool of hot liquid, and he was a fish looking for a place to swim. The pool wasn't even a fucking option right now. Not that it had even been an option before. Because he was running out of those, and he was headed down a street without a final destination—the third punch, the one that knocked him on his ass, notwithstanding.

The strange man had even knocked Johnny's cowboy hat off his head. It had ended up on the ground next to him, flipped over on the brim. And Johnny thought he might have been missing a tooth, but that was a false alarm.

Every patron had turned in the other direction, and the blonde that had shown more than a little interest before had lost her attentiveness. She discreetly looked away and focused on the trashy romance novel in front of her face. Looking back, he probably shouldn't have been all that proud of himself. But he was.

To keep his pride in check, though, he needed to forget the recent past, or he'd end up flat on his ass all over again. That was one performance he didn't plan to repeat.

∽∾∽

Gwendoline had a beer in one hand and a fork in the other. The fork danced through her fingertips, clattering against the plate, and coming to rest just outside her grasp. She hadn't expected him. He was damn sure not supposed to be in this particular picture. Her head had swelled up to twice its normal size, and her heart pounded up against the back of her throat. Her voice was constricted, nonexistent, and she was certain that she would somehow have to face the music.

Gwendoline hadn't seen Johnny Chapman in over two years, and those two years had been the longest of her life. The change of pace slowed from a run to a crawl, and she found herself craving an intensity that she had never managed to recapture. His intensity. Her world had revolved around him once, and she vowed to never let it happen again.

She could have jumped right in, if she really stopped to think about it, but she was a spectator, staring from a distance, standing on the edge of a precipice, and she was about to dive over the edge, duck her head underwater, and leave it there until the bubbles stopped and her world ended. It might have been easier to leave all her problems before she had to face them and deal with hopeful appreciation or a single complication. Maybe it was the complications she needed to worry about the most.

Maybe it was his charm that got to her. Maybe it was his charm that left her hoping for something more. Maybe his problems led her to a few more solutions. But even if his problems proved helpful, she might not find them particularly useful. His situation held a need and desire for her: the desire to do better, achieve more, reach out, and touch some significant precipice, some anatomical desire that had captured her at the most basic level. Johnny, the man at the bar, held such a desire for her, a growing need that she couldn't control nor could she explain it, but she needed to contain it before it was too late.

All of it was out of hand. Gwendoline took a drink. And then another. Each drink offered up a steady state, a calm wave, the closing of one life and the beginning of another. A more fulfilled and happy life. The life from two years ago, not the life she experienced right now.

The alcohol hit her in waves. The tide crashed and surrounded her, as the blackness closed in and nearly suffocated her. Divine intervention somehow controlled her very existence, even as her existence needed some sort of to-do list.

The past needed an explanation, otherwise she would end up painted in a corner, with her back against the wall and the man on the other side of the bar making her feel incomplete and unfulfilled. Her life lacked even the most basic participation. Her needs were cold and calculated and possibly even nonexistent, and hope checked a box right before the next item on her list.

Her life built from the moments that preceded it. And

this was one particular instance she wished would just go away.

ℰℐℰℐ

Johnny didn't have to do it. But he wanted to. He wanted to lift his arms up high over his head and keep his dreams firmly planted in the clouds. And he might have had a good run. Who was to say for sure? He might have tried just a little bit harder, he might have given just a little bit more, but the bitch was here. In his memories. Sucking up the remainder of his reality. Every time he tried to move forward, he ended up taking a step back and dancing with the devil on the hardwood floor.

If he hadn't managed to give it his all, he might have ended up with more than a broken lip and a busted jaw. The man had blended in with the crowd and ended up on the other side of the bar, chatting away with the blonde he had set his sights on.

When Johnny's pride returned, she was there. In the shadows. Leaning against the wall. Her hands at her side, her face turned in an upward direction, one eye scowling at him, and the other turned away from him. The eye that was on him watched his every move, saw his every flaw, and poked at his heart with a chainsaw. She had big eyes. The largest he had ever seen. Hungry eyes. That was what he told her once. And he would have told her again if she hadn't walked out the door on him. He had been the one staring up at the ceiling. His fist clenched, his eyes shut, his breathing coming rapidly, so rapidly that he nearly passed out. He unclenched his heart, held it so tightly against his chest that he thought it might explode. That was what she did to him. And she did it over and over again. Haunting his memories so much that he came to expect it after a while, so used to it that he thought something was seriously wrong with him when it didn't happen. When none of it happened, he was ready to dive into the water, have it envelop him, consume him, and maybe even control him.

Gwendoline had controlled him. Every single thought. To the point that it had nearly swallowed him whole. To the point that he fished without a pole, his feet shoved into the edge of the water, as he held one hand away from his chest, while the other flicked his wrist, casting out that imaginary line of hope and consternation and aggravation.

The man had messed with his priorities. A burning sensation filled his chest. And Johnny shook his head, jerking away from the errant thought that had taken over his world. Absence might have given him what he needed. Or then again, it might not.

He met Gwendoline after he had slid into home plate at an awkward angle and nearly broken his knee in two. It had required three surgeries to repair the knee, and he still didn't have full and complete use of it. It ached like a son of a bitch, and he walked with a limp. The damn catcher had a smirk on his face as he crowded the plate and prepared for the oncoming collision. And Johnny had just lain there, staring up into the lights and stars, as the moon winked at him. The past had been wonderful and meaningful, and then it had been nothing at all. No one wanted to touch him. Told him he was damaged goods. That he was washed up and washed out.

A year later, she had done the same.

He didn't smirk. He lost his swagger. And then he didn't really have much at all. His life ended the moment she walked out the front door.

The instant the bottle came to his lips, it drowned out the pain and the heartache and the despair. It had been because he wanted it, because he craved the numbness, the emptiness, and then he had needed it.

He couldn't live without the bottle. Or that's what he'd been led to believe.

She had approached him from the other side of the bar with a hand on her hip and a swagger in her step and three-inch heels on her feet. He had three bottles in front of him, and he was working his way through a fourth.

"If you take one more drink, I'm walking out," Gwendoline said.

He had nodded his head and shoved the remainder of the bottle out of his way.

That was how it ended. The drinking. It wasn't any more complicated than that. It might have been tragic if it wasn't so instrumental in his downfall.

When she left him, he returned to the bottle once more, only this time the hole was bigger than it was before.

ꙮꙮꙮ

Gwendoline glared at him from the other side of the room, and then she marched in his direction, filled with sass and pure determination. Both her hands were empty, but her right one was closed into a fist, while her left one was stiff at her side. The crowd parted for her, and a few men stared at her backside. The beat blasted through speakers that hummed with instrumental feedback, while a voice in the crowd roared with pure determination.

Her dark hair stood away from her face, and her outfit was tight in all the right places. She wore flats on her feet and a stern expression on her face. She tapped the bar beside him before she commandeered the stool to his left.

Tossing normal pleasantries out the window, she focused on the heart of the matter. "You can shove it up your ass," Gwendoline said.

"I don't think it'll fit."

Her right elbow bumped against his side. "Just what exactly are you trying to prove?"

Johnny shrugged. "Maybe nothing. Maybe something. How have you been?"

Her energy cut through the distance between them. A drink appeared before her. She slammed her head back and drank it down.

"I'm rather good with a gun. You don't want to test me."

His eyes flicked in an upward motion. "That's for damn sure."

"But you don't think I'll do it?"

"You walked out on me once, and I know you'd be more than happy to do it again."

She rolled her shoulders and adjusted her position. "You never did anything."

It was true, he hadn't. But then again, she had caught him by surprise with her suitcase in one hand and her backpack in the other. And when she walked out the door, she hadn't even said a word, but the extreme intensity on her face cut him down more than her words ever would have.

He had spent the next two years trying to rediscover normal.

CHAPTER 4

Gwendoline had a corner office on the sixth floor overlooking a trash compactor and a dumpster. A Flying Star across the street provided her comfort when the sludge being pumped from the automatic coffee machine caused her heartburn. Streaks filled her window and her view, and she jammed a folded piece of paper underneath the front right leg of her desk, otherwise her world was continually off balance.

Seeing Johnny the night before had pushed her equilibrium in the wrong direction, and the Post-it note plastered to the front of her screen made her otherwise queasy stomach even more uneasy. The note was unsigned, but it was no secret her boss had placed it there and continued his early morning rounds.

Fridays were generally quiet days, with half the staff either working from home or off in anticipation of a longer-than-normal weekend. Her weekends were never longer than normal, and, in most instances, much shorter than she would have preferred. Despite her office being a corner one, it was one of the smallest she had ever encountered.

Since she was still working on her first cup of coffee, Gwendoline gave herself a few minutes to collect her thoughts before she funneled upstairs to see the man behind the cherry desk with the haphazard stare and attention span.

She finished her early morning coffee and calisthenics, adjusted her blouse and bra, and checked her makeup with the hand mirror in her bottom drawer. She followed one deep breath up with another, dragged her chair back, and concentrated on whatever fate might bring her today.

Leonardo Nivea waved her inside and motioned for her to close the door. He didn't offer her a seat, so she stood. When he mentioned the conversation wouldn't take long, she believed him. He was a man of few words and even fewer expressions. Other than lifting his arm, Leonardo made no other movements with the rest of his body.

When the silence lingered, it didn't turn uncomfortable, but leeriness entered the air. Even the empty walls stared at her, judged her, and made her feel even smaller than she already did.

Until Leonardo told her she was being let go.

"What do you mean I'm fired?"

Pleasantries were not a particular affinity for him.

"It's not difficult to comprehend. If you need me to draw you a roadmap—"

"That's just it," she said. "You haven't told me anything. What the hell's going on?"

Leonardo pushed a stack of forms in her direction. "This conversation is over."

She held up a hand. "Wait. Can't you at least tell me why?"

Her whole career flashed before her eyes: the long hours, the short weekends, the missed lunches and dinners, and a social network that was currently on life support. For an instant, Johnny entered her thought process as well.

Leonardo's eyes focused on a spot above her head. "No. I'm sorry."

She stared so hard her world began to fragment and blur. "But you're really not."

"Maybe not, maybe so."

The paperwork lingered on the edge of his desk, perfectly balanced, and hovering just out of her reach.

"You really are a bastard."

He pushed the forms headfirst in her direction. "That's not the first time those five words have been uttered in my presence."

She leaned forward and snatched the paperwork with her right hand.

Leonardo placed his hand over the top of hers, and she jerked it back with the paperwork still intact.

"You shouldn't have done that."

The distance between them disappeared. With her head still ringing, Gwendoline made her decision, and, in hindsight, it probably wasn't the right one.

The punch landed squarely on his jaw. And when Leonardo hit the floor, he might have seen an ex-girlfriend, a ghost, or maybe the gates of Hell. He jerked once and went still, and she turned her head away before he decided to regain consciousness.

∽∾∽

With a goon on either side of her, and sunglasses covering their chiseled faces, she piled six years of her life into two boxes the size of milk cartons. Gwendoline had fifteen minutes to pack, and she completed her task in less than fourteen minutes. She bent over at the waist at one point, instead of bending with her knees, her short skirt riding up the back of her thighs, and not so much as a cough out of the gentleman on her right or her left.

She crammed both boxes to the brink of exploding, and she still had plenty of items without a cardboard home. With nary a glance in either direction, she couldn't even offer up a cardboard cutout smile. She smashed her handheld mirror on the corner of her desk, and the two goons dragged her from her office with a hand on each elbow, as her heels slammed against the plush red carpet. Her grim expression remained in the on position, and her head bobbed faster with each passing second. The boxes were dropped on the curb, along with her. She turned and gave the concrete façade the one-fingered salute for the last time. Pinching her right palm, she held back the tears and redirected the pain for what was the final time.

A teenager on a cell phone mowed her down, and her knee struck the pavement at an awkward angle. She cursed under her breath, her gaze penetrating the back of his head. No apology was forthcoming as she pushed herself to her feet and rubbed her knee. She adjusted her skirt, grabbed one of the milk cartons, and shoved herself in the direction of her car.

Her heels clicked on the pavement and images ran through her mind three at a time. Her heart leaped in her chest, and the carton leaped in her hand. Nothing about the last twenty-four hours felt right after she had spotted Johnny from across the room and tunneled her focus in his direction.

Soon, a string of words had followed along with her, and she felt the distinctive presence of male breath on the back of her neck.

"I don't want to relive the past," Johnny said.

Her head whipped around, and she dropped the carton on her big toe. She grimaced and bit her tongue. "You haven't changed at all."

He had been following her, but she didn't know for how long. She had no idea if he had seen her cry. But fighting for her life became her number one priority.

He picked up the cardboard container and handed it to her. "I need to move on."

"Is that why you drive by my house at night?"

His car had slowed to a stop and paused outside her front door. Gwendoline had considered calling the cops before she lost the thought and closed the curtains. Becoming one with the darkness had been her best move at the time, and it had paid off. Ten seconds later he had driven away.

He took a step toward her and reached out a hand. She slapped it away.

Johnny's head jerked. "That only happened once."

"Is that why you follow me?"

His face hardened and then softened. She clung to the box with both hands and turned her head in the direction of her destination. The sound of a car horn momentarily shifted her focus. He touched her shoulder, and she knocked his hand away with her elbow.

His smirk entered her world. "If it bothers you, why don't you move?"

"Why should I be the one to uproot my life?" Her

pause was as brief as his stare. "You're one flamboyant bastard."

He shrugged and pointed at the box in her hands. "It grows more beautiful the longer you hold onto it."

Gwendoline glared. "Did you read that in a book?"

"Maybe. But the ones with pictures are my favorite."

She shifted the box in her grasp. "Do you like it?"

"What?"

"Being an asshole."

The grin on his face widened. "Not really."

"Now I know you're lying." She pushed herself forward with both feet. "Did I already tell you that you're a bastard?"

"Probably at some point," Johnny replied. "But then you've never refrained from driving home a particular point when the opportunity presented itself."

Since she had no immediate response to his, she continued forward without bothering to look back.

❧❦❧

The good life might have passed him by. Or maybe it was a figment of his imagination. Maybe it was some dream on some horizon that was just out of reach, pushing and pulling him, and bouncing him around like a red rubber ball on an open field. The ride of his life had ended in chaos, or maybe it was a fiery wreck on the side of the highway, as the cops showed up, followed by an ambulance, and the paramedics exiting the white van on the side of the road.

Johnny had watched her walk away once, and now her skirt twitched as she did it again. He flicked his index finger against his wrist, flipped his hand over, and stared at his watch. He hadn't expected to run into her again in less than twenty-four hours. The sidewalk hadn't been big enough for the both of them, just as his world hadn't been big enough for her.

Walking out on him once had hurt, and now the open wound was rubbed raw once again. Her smile had lit up his world before she'd covered it with darkness and locusts. His head still rang from the drinking and thinking the night before, and a dull ache stuck to the front of his forehead.

He'd seen it too many times already, being fired, walking the streets, looking for his next drink, seeking out his next sloppy partner with no thought whatsoever as to what that might mean to her. That had been his world, not hers.

Johnny whistled as he walked in the opposite direction of Gwendoline, and he picked up his knees with each step, the muscles taut and tight and angry. A gift from his playing days when the fields were green, and his vision was long.

Baseball had been his life. And now it wasn't. He

could have gone pro. Or that's what three scouts had told him, two of which had since retired.

He had placed one foot in front of the other, and he'd made it to the head of the pack. The leader. And he'd watched it all slip out of his hands. He'd lost his head and his emotions in equal measure, and he'd spent the rest of the year riding the pine and watching kids with less talent take the spot that should have been his. His butt had shifted on that bench more times than he'd care to admit, and he'd spoken out, but no one had heard his pleas, and he'd stared up at a world that shifted around him. Something within him had died that first day and every day thereafter. Even hope proved condescending, as it offered up a smile and a wink before it punched him in the gut and stole his lunch money.

He continued around the corner and out of her purview and punched the wall. The stucco cut across his knuckles, ripping skin, and he punched it again. He pulled his hand away and stared at the dripping blood that smacked the concrete and splattered in an uneven pattern.

Women had been the extent of his demise. Like the blonde in high school with the brilliant smile and the perky breasts, and the never-ending legs, and the bluest eyes that he'd ever seen. He had been stupid then, and he was stupid now. Both times he focused his gaze on the back of their heads.

ℰↄℰↄ

But this time she came back for her other cardboard box on the sidewalk. Johnny wiped his knuckles with his left hand and brushed the red on the side of his jeans. He smiled, but her expression remained in the neutral position. Her walk was filled with purpose and poise, and she shoved past him with the back of her hand.

Gwendoline shook with rage. "You really are a bastard."

"I thought we already covered this." Her skirt hugged her thighs, and he couldn't turn his gaze away as sweat trickled down his chin.

She bent at the knees and picked up the box. "Maybe we're going to cover it again."

He wiped his hands on the front of his shirt. The sound of a crying toddler momentarily distracted him, and when he turned his head around, she had already turned away from his face.

"That skirt clings to you in all the right places."

Her head whipped around, and her eyes narrowed. The box in her hands dropped an inch, and she clung to it even tighter. "You really are a stupid piece of shit."

He shrugged his shoulders and grabbed the box from her outstretched hands. "Your car's around the corner, isn't it?"

She nodded. "I like it that way. It helps me keep my distance from your overbearing personality. You might want to tone it down just a tad."

"You know, some women find me charming," Johnny said.

Her head shook followed by her shoulders. "That's not the reason. But if you continue to tell yourself that, you might start to believe it."

"You know, you're going to discover you can't live without me."

"No, I'm going to find out that you're still a bastard. Two years might have changed me, but I think you're still the same person you were back then."

He shrugged. "Probably."

Gwendoline lunged for the box, and he pulled his hands and his body in the opposite direction. "I never did find that particularly endearing. Or you for that matter."

He noticed the slight hint of hurt and emptiness in her eyes, and if not for the box in his hands, he would have touched her shoulder.

His eyes softened. "You might not believe it now, but we did have one motherfucking good time."

This time when she lunged for the box, he let her have it.

სოცი

Johnny waited for her on the sidewalk for close to twenty minutes, but she never did come back.

The bar was not far from his present location. The

tinted windows were a dead giveaway toward the hidden treasures that lay inside. The door was tall and dark and sturdy, and the man with his eyes on the street was tall and lanky with long, dark hair that dripped into his eyes. His shirt was trimmed away at his shoulder blades, and his jeans were two sizes too big and held at the waist with a large belt and buckle. He flicked his fingers in a back and forth motion, and Johnny stepped toward him.

With his ID checked, the door opened, the ringing in his ears increased, lights flashed, and a woman took the bills from his outstretched hand. A bracelet was slapped around his wrist, a brief smile was offered in his direction, and a flash of tanned skin caught the corner of his eye. His soles banged against the linoleum, and he lifted his chin at the sound of a feminine voice. The huskiness cut through to his core, and he gnawed at his cheek as he focused his head in her direction.

Johnny should have seen her coming, the blonde wig and the darkened skin, but he had been blind to the good times. Or he had been blind to something more serious with a woman named Gwendoline Pearce. An overwhelming sensation nearly threatened to crush him from the inside out. A roundabout feeling that was going to send him over the edge and drop him into the water several hundred feet below.

She told him her name was Clover without the three additional leaves, and she offered him a wink when she asked for his drink. Her outfit was light green and sheer, and she shimmied her hips as she palmed the notepad against her bronzed skin. Her eyes were deep green and might have been colored contacts. She cupped her hip with her other hand, her arm jutting out at the elbow, and when he smiled, she cocked her hip.

All legs and tits and ass. If she wasn't a porn star, she had damn sure missed her calling. He was so hard he thought his eyes were going to pop out of his head, and she'd barely glanced at his face. Instead, she had chosen a point just off to the side of his head. Probably on purpose. He hated to lose control, to run in about six different directions at once, and end up in the middle of nowhere.

Johnny ordered two club sodas and took a booth far away from the stage. The platform was lit up like the Fourth of July. The girl moved with an ease and comfort all her own. She was all sensation and stilettos. Music pounded in his ears, and he probably drooled at one point. The song ended, but she didn't. She kept moving, effortlessly and endlessly, and he tried not to stare. Tried and failed miserably. His two drinks came, but he hardly noticed.

Another song started, and her top slipped from her shoulders. Moving and shaking and endlessly taking whatever she wanted. The beat pounded faster, and her body twisted and twirled around the stage. An endless whirlwind of emotion. She grabbed the pole with her outstretched arms and inched up it before sliding down. Bending her body toward the audience, and the tips of her nipples pointed at the hairy man in the front row with a stack of bills over an inch tall.

Johnny hated her. And he wanted her. The conflicting emotions caught him off guard. He pounded one of his drinks down and slipped his hand toward the other. But before he could take hold of the glass, he slammed his fist against his forehead.

A sea of emptiness had taken control of his world and left him with nothing. Nothing was what he was feeling now. Nothing and everything at the same time. He shifted in his seat, and the booth sighed in response. He grabbed the other drink and slammed it back, the glass clicking against his teeth. He dropped the empty crystal to the table, and it flipped over on its side.

He had lost control over even his basic faculties, but she certainly hadn't. He'd been so focused on her body that he had neglected her face. When he finally turned his attention in that particular direction, his head jerked back and slammed against the mirror. The thud jolted him out of his fantasy, but no one else seemed to notice.

He'd seen her before. But where? He racked his brain, rubbed his forehead, cycled through the last three years of his life, and came up empty-handed. He had six pennies in his pocket and a wad of cash. Mostly fives and ones. An ATM card with a bank balance in the three-digit range called out to him as loud as the stripper on the stage.

In short, he was fucked. And he wasn't even going to get the chance to enjoy it.

And she knew it. For the first time, she looked in his direction and stared right through him as she gyrated against the pole, her toned legs and arms humping and pumping. The music banged louder and louder as the rapper was drowned out by a syncopated rhythm. It was all over in a fiery storm of passion that left Johnny's mind on the stage and his thoughts in the gutter.

He stood up and brushed off his pants, closed his eyes, and tried to capture the last sensation that entered his brain. Wildflowers and jasmine. A scent coming from behind him. A wonderful sensation that made him feel nothing, and offered him hope and need, and brought him back from the abyss. The texture passed right through him, and he was back in a sensual experience that discounted his thoughts on more than one level.

When she touched his shoulder and whispered in his ear, his insides turned to slush.

❦❧❦

"I'm Eden." She stuck out her hand, and the band around her wrist twirled.

He shook it. "Johnny."

Her hand touched the small of his back, and he shivered. Even when he didn't look at her, he could feel her smile. She whispered some random phrase in his ear, and his body jerked in response. Her breasts were less than an inch away from the side of his face, and he could hear the fabric move every time she shifted position. She managed to do it more often than not.

Warm breath attacked his ear. "Do you like sunsets?"

"Who doesn't?" he asked. "It means another day in the bag."

Her breasts leaned in closer. "Maybe it means a new beginning is waiting."

If he received any more surprises, he might end up in a ditch on the side of the road with a hammer stuck to the back of his skull. Possibly by her boyfriend who could toss him across the room just for fun.

Johnny leaned back. "Are you going for some kind of award?"

Her breath reached the back of his neck, and he shivered harder. When he asked her what she wanted, she didn't offer up a reply.

"Nothing sounds pretty damn wonderful right about now," he said.

He felt her smile before he noticed it.

CHAPTER 5

The wind pulsed around him, cutting through him faster than a blade. Tumbleweed blew across his path, and silence managed to fill the void. The scraping sound surrounded him, closing in, ready to suffocate, and add to his world in equal installments. He was on his knees in the sand. She was looking down at him, ready to invade his world, ready to offer up her soul to him, and she looked away. Her eyes flicked toward the distance where small bushes and cacti filled a unique pattern across an open field.

Johnny stared out at a sea of passion, of crashing waves and surrounding bliss, and he was left feeling effortless, floating on the brink of some sense of greatness that was more than ready to swallow him whole.

He had felt a sense of promise, of desperation, and

his hand had shaken when she had taken his in her own.

Her shift ended early, Eden had told him, and he had followed her blindly. Obediently. He would have followed her firm ass anywhere, and all it had taken was one smile and a few whispered promises. He had handed over the last of his cash and followed her into the back room where she had bumped and ground against his knees. Then she had asked him to wait for her out back where there was only the light of a distant moon to guide him. And Johnny had done it because he was in a trance filled with circumstance, and he had turned off whatever voice might have held his emotions in check.

With the last of his instinct suppressed, he had given in to the demons inside of him. Her clothes were baggy, and her hair was pulled away from her face. Her eyes were bigger than the rest of her, and she hadn't glanced once in his direction, as she led him away from his vehicle and out into the middle of nowhere. A flock of black circled overhead, and the heat from the sun smacked him in the face. Mountains rose in the distance, and a string of volcanoes zeroed in on the back of his head.

A phone call was made, and a voice answered on the other end. Words were exchanged, and his fate remained in the hands of a woman with a pair of enormous breasts that were more than covered by her billowing top. None of it seemed real—not the car ride, or the woman by his side, or the sun, or the wind, or the green and blue lizards crawling across his shoes, or the roadrunner with the tuft of blue hair sticking out from the top of his head as he dashed across the sand.

She turned back to him—Eden, not the roadrunner—and bit her lower lip. Her eyes were bright and filled with a depth of knowledge that he had never quite expected. Her gaze flicked away to the mountains in the distance and the roadrunner that had darted in search of his new home. Moments of his life flashed before his eyes. A highlight reel filled with salted peanuts and combed sand and metal benches and beautiful women and a mixing bowl of emotions.

Her look that was only there for an instant was hope-ful and meaningful and, all at once, he was ready to for-give her, and hope that his fate wouldn't play out similar to a roulette wheel.

One woman, and he'd been completely lost, caught up in a moment on stage that had soon departed. He'd held onto the image in the back of his mind to the point that he had blindly followed her to her car and never stopped to question what might have motivated her.

౿Ⴢ౿Ⴢ

Eden hated him. The thought struck her instantly and overwhelmed her to the point that she sank to her knees. Worse than even her last ex-boyfriend. The one who thought beating her was a form of survival and, somehow, proved he loved her even more. The temper tantrums were reminiscent of a two-year-old who hadn't managed to get his way. He had lashed out at her with his fists and the back of his hand, and he had broken her spirit down to a shell of her former self. It had taken months of counseling before she was finally able to gain her life back.

When she'd finally had the courage to walk away from him, she'd ended up with a broken leg and arm for her trouble. At least he hadn't broken her nose. She didn't know how she'd survive, or continue to dance, if he had.

When she stood up, she brushed off her black slacks. She and men didn't exactly get along. Not even close. It was a combustible exercise filled with trauma and drama and, when it was all over, she felt so exhausted that hibernation was the only way she could recharge her batteries. Instant attraction was a drug, and she was addicted ever since she turned fifteen. That bad boy with the glint in his eye and more than a hint of wildness beneath those long dark lashes pulled at her insides like some magnetic force. And every boy turned out to be a bastard.

No exceptions.

A tear trickled down her face, and she swiped it away. She gritted her teeth and shoved her phone into her pocket.

She had been told five minutes, but it'd probably end up closer to ten.

Her lips burned from where he kissed her. It had been a fleeting moment. An instant. An impulsive reaction to an emotional response. And now she was on the sand and gravel, staring down at him, and ready to swallow her lower lip before the next misbegotten emotion swept over her. Suddenly, she couldn't breathe. The air around her was thick with heat, and her gaze shifted toward the red and orange sky.

Before she could think twice, she punched him in the face and screamed. Her own voice rocked through her, and she managed to shake her head and smile at the same time. The end was so close she wanted to grasp it. Men had managed to control her life for years, and she was finally ready to take back what remained of it.

She punched him again. And screamed again. Not as hard this time, or as loud. But it felt good. Great, actually. Her emotional response overwhelmed her, and she collapsed to the ground with her knees plastered in the sand. She was somehow free. Johnny would allow her to cut the cord and move on with her life.

Only, this time, she'd dance in the right direction.

e∂e∂

None of it felt tangible—the punching, or the

screaming, or the jab on the back of his neck and the slip into unconsciousness. Blackness passed before him, and he dropped to the sand.

The dream continued indefinitely. From one moment to the next, it carried each thought away. Each second captured between two sodden pages. The words captured and repeated and revealed. A bell chimed in the distance. A hand clasped around Johnny's throat, and he saw only darkness. Drifting off or drifting down below the surface, he sensed hope needling at the back of his mind. The sands of time moved forward, even as he drifted to the surface.

It was now dark where it had been light before. The fluorescent light overhead mocked him, and his eyes widened at the figure above him. The man was unfamiliar and as large as a door. Compassion had left the man's face long ago, and sadness had filled in a void or two. Johnny blinked, but that didn't make the lights dim, nor did it make the figure go away. The chair was hard beneath him. Solid. His hands were tied behind his back, and a piece of wood was jammed just below his shoulder blade.

His feet shifted on the concrete beneath him, and a scraping sound cut through the light. The lamp flickered down at him.

The bell chimed again. A grandfather clock. Or maybe a church bell. Maybe he was in a basement or an unfinished house. Maybe the street was familiar to him, or maybe it wasn't.

His watch had been removed from his wrist. His bound hands shifted with the movement of the chair, and, still, the figure loomed above him, glaring and staring and reaching out to adjust his seat back into a similar position on the concrete floor.

Johnny squinted at the harsh light. "What the hell is going on?"

"Did you think you could run from us?"

The voice sounded familiar, but he didn't have a face to go with the man. Disorientation had set his brain on edge, or maybe it was the woman that was no longer near him. He should have never trusted a woman, especially a beautiful one with plump lips.

"I wasn't aware I was running."

Harrison stepped into the light. "Then what were you doing?"

"Surviving," Johnny said. "It's what I do best."

Harrison cracked his knuckles. "You're an idiot."

"I've been called worse."

A hand reached out and gripped his neck. "How could you lose our money?"

Johnny coughed and sputtered and flailed in the chair. "I t—thought it was a sure thing. The girl c—cheated."

Harrison's face turned red, and his voice rose.

"You're going to bring her into it." A hand reached out for his neck again. "Do you think that will change your predicament?"

Johnny glared and flailed. "It's t—true. She was c— counting cards, reading hands."

Harrison pulled his hand away, and his eyes narrowed. "How would you know?"

Johnny smiled. "Her lips were moving."

"That doesn't make you any less of an idiot," Harrison said. "Maybe she was talking to herself. Your luck with women has taken on something of a losing streak."

Johnny rubbed his wrists against the back of the chair. The ties held, and his wrists turned slick. "I play the same table every week."

"And you lose every week."

Johnny grinned. "I'm about to find my winning streak."

Harrison took a step forward, but his hands remained at his sides. "You're always on the verge of a winning streak. Filling your head with lies doesn't lead to the truth."

"No," Johnny said, "but it makes me feel better."

"Do not test me."

One moment of silence bled into another. A bell chimed once and was silent again. The two male statues stood at attention.

Harrison adjusted his shirt collar before he undid the

top button. "You really don't know what any of this is about, do you?"

Johnny shook his head. "No, but I have a feeling you're going to tell me."

Harrison turned his back to Johnny. When he turned around, he held a needle in his previously empty hand. Johnny's eyes flicked from the needle to the man and back again. The metal glimmered in the light, and a bit of liquid ejected from the tip.

The needle danced between Harrison's hands. "We have a race you need to fix."

Johnny couldn't turn his gaze away, nor could he focus his attention on anything other than the plastic and long metal spike. "What?"

Harrison dropped the needle on the metal table. "There's a dog—"

Johnny's hands banged against the back of the chair, and he squirmed to the right. "What dog?"

"A winner," Harrison replied. "This race—he won't win."

"Are you serious?"

Harrison's lips shifted. "As chlamydia."

The silence lingered for several moments. Johnny had always liked dogs, along with animals in general. But his mom had never offered him more than a guinea pig.

"You're a psycho."

Harrison stepped forward, reached out his hands, and

squeezed. "You can die now." Another pause lingered on, while he pulled his hands away. "Or do this job for us." He shrugged. "It makes no difference to me."

Johnny shifted his weight once more. Harrison grabbed his legs.

"You want me to kill a dog?"

"I want you to inject a dog," Harrison said. "We'll give you the hormones."

Johnny tilted his head to the side. "You want me to inject a dog with hormones so he doesn't win a race? What the hell kind of hormones are we talking about?"

"Good hormones," Harrison replied. "We tested them out on you."

Johnny's eyes searched the room, looking for a way out. But all he saw were cracks and cobwebs and concrete. A stone pillar stood between the otherwise mute men.

He'd kept his body free of alcohol and nicotine for damn near six months, and now he had some hormone floating around in his system doing who knew what. He hated the arrogant prick in front of him with every mole on his skin.

"I've been drugged?"

Harrison looked at his watch. The gold glinted in the light. "So are you in or are you out?"

Johnny rubbed his hands up and down even more furiously. "Do I have a choice in the matter?"

"You always have a choice," Harrison said. "But will you make the right one?"

CHAPTER 6

Johnny had the glint of confidence in his eyes, and he stared right through Harrison and his thousand-dollar suit. "Are you going to make me an offer I can't refuse?"

"No," Harrison said, "but I am going to kill you if you fail in this mission."

Johnny stared even harder. Harrison was the first to look away. "Is that a threat?"

"You and I both know I don't make threats."

He should have asked for a refund or a whimsical glare with a thousand-dollar stare. At least a promise of what might have been. Instead, Johnny was all out of promises and circumstances and second chances. It was all so easy to lose. He'd left it all behind—most of his money and the better part of his hide—at some point, and he was out of opportunities to gain it all back.

He'd been cut loose, let go. For now. The ties slipped off, and he slipped to his feet. He rubbed his knees and his chaffing wrists. The two men had left Harrison's side. Johnny was alone with what was left of his emotions. The electricity had been shut off, and his eyes adjusted to the dark. He'd made a deal with the devil when he agreed to inject that stupid dog. He pictured a mutt with a wagging tail and tongue, and eyes that reminded him of a child.

He rubbed his wrists—the blood had partially dried—and found his sea legs again after sitting in a chair for four hours, staring at the fluorescent light, staring at a spot on the wall six inches above his head, staring at a face filled with emptiness.

His mind drifted and shifted. He found his happiness back on the mound. Pitching with the bases loaded and a full count staring back at him, and the best hitter from the opposition winking in his direction. The batter had already fouled off two sliders, so he was seven pitches into an opposing duel. Johnny had already surrendered a double and a single to this bastard, and he wasn't about to do it all again. The catcher gave him the sign for a curve, and Johnny considered it for just a moment, ready to wave it off, but then he decided that it was the pitch he needed. The bastard at the plate always had trouble with the curve, and Johnny's was a thing of beauty, dropping a good six inches before it crossed the plate. He would strike this bastard out, even if it was the last thing he ever did.

Johnny popped up, walked the ball around in his glove, found the grip that suited him best, found the right spot on the mound, his spot, stared straight ahead, just playing catch in the field, as he blocked out the roaring crowd, the cheers and jeers in the background, and the constant comments from the other bench. The noise. He shrugged his shoulders, loosened up his arms, cleared his mind of all thought and emotion, and focused on this particular instant that would live forever in his mind. He wound up, his arms forming a T motion, and let the ball fly.

ↄ/ↄↄ/ↄ

Harrison had a phone in one hand, and a massive tit in the other from a woman currently of his employ. Her IQ couldn't have been much north of seventy, but she could fuck like a porn star. He had discovered this the last time his wife was out of town, and he had filled the woman with four glasses of poolside champagne. Not long afterward she had shed her clothes, dove into the water, emerged, and dripped all over his concrete deck. Every time he thought about this scenario, he ended up with a massive hard-on.

Thinking of Johnny Chapman and his penchant for

losing money managed to cure him of said hard-on, and if Johnny couldn't come through, he'd enjoy watching the lights go out over New Mexico.

The man on the other end of the line was a bit higher on the social ladder, and wasn't much of a gambler, except when it came to absolute certainties. He believed in zero risk, but he also had over a million dollars currently stuffed in a Cayman Islands bank account, and that was just his walking around money. Harrison hated the fucker, but he was a necessary evil. The conversation had started with trophy wives and fine wines before he dove right in. Small talk was fine, as long as it was less than four minutes long.

"What makes you so sure this is going to work out?"

Harrison grabbed the phone tighter. "Do you really want to know?"

"That bastard of a dog has won six races in a row."

Harrison rubbed the taut pink nipple with his left hand before he switched to the other tit. The woman, always eager to please, accommodated his concerted effort. "True. But he's won his last race."

"What the hell do you mean?"

"Just trust me," Harrison said.

"The last time I trusted you I was five figures in the hole and staring at a bed of roses on the top of my grave. If it hadn't been for the Albanian—"

The Albanian was a hitman of an entirely different

flavor. He had nine fingers—no left pinky—and two scars on his left bicep and one on his right. For the highest bidder, he was a ruthless killer with an inferiority complex.

Harrison rubbed her nipple harder. "Don't be so melodramatic."

"Drama is good for the soul," the man said.

"Says the man devoid of all drama." As far as Harrison knew, the man had never even cheated on his wife. He was a boy scout with too much money and power, and no particular outlet to alleviate either one.

"I always manage to find it when I want it."

"What do you want now?" Harrison asked.

"I want to leave all my troubles behind."

"A song title?"

"A famous verse," the man said. "You don't read much, do you?"

Writers were pompous shits with grandiose plans and tendencies. If he could, he'd kill every one of the stupid fuckers. "So are you playing or not?"

"I'll get back to you."

"You might not want to wait too long," Harrison said. "This plan has a definite expiration date. By the way, you might want to update your yacht. The cedar floors were looking a little scuffed."

"That's what you said the last time, too."

"At least I'm consistent," Harrison said.

He ended the call and started up another. Several conversations later—most of which had similar results— he ceased the tit grabbing, bent his secretary over his desk, lifted up her skirt, and fucked her from behind. Afterward, he forced her to clean up and ordered her to go home.

 espaço

She'd been consistent in her choice of men. And that consistency had placed Gwendoline smack dab in the middle of her present predicament. She'd faced a certain amount of indignity in her life. Remembrance managed to smack her on the ass and shove a loaded weapon down the back of her throat.

The table was off center, her meal was overcooked, her date was five years older than his profile said he was, and her hair had somehow gone amiss between her house and the restaurant. No amount of concealer could alleviate the pimple on her chin. A giant boar hung overhead, she wanted to strangle the waiter with the high-pitched voice, the place was covered in pastel pinks and yellows, and the stool was jammed against the crack of her ass. At least the green chile was hot enough to burn her tongue.

Her date systematically shoved food into his mouth. And she'd hardly touched hers. She'd hardly felt much of anything. His smile was awkward, his handshake was off, and his voice was deeper than she would have liked. The bald spot on his head wasn't doing him any favors either. And there was something about what remained of his hair that she found annoying, but she couldn't pinpoint the specific issue.

The conversation had taken a turn for the worse about ten minutes ago, but she still had what was left of her social graces.

Gwendoline rubbed the end of her nose. "What the hell are you looking at?"

"Do you always stare off when you're thinking?"

"Force of habit." Daydreaming had never been a problem for her.

"What other habits do you have?"

"You don't want to know." She'd killed a man once, but he'd deserved it.

"I like to pretend my life started in college. Before that, it's filled with bad memories and troubling circumstances."

Her life was one giant memory she preferred to forget. Death didn't bring her justice, but she had hoped life would. She'd gotten fucked on that deal as well. "Somewhere along the way, it's all relative."

"Only in West Virginia."

Gwendoline rubbed the end of her nose again. "I thought it was South Dakota."

He shrugged and slammed his fork against his plate.
"I guess it depends on where you grew up."

ᔮᔭᔮ

Johnny had a black eye. The rat bastard had smacked
him good. His cheek still throbbed, and it'd probably
throb into tomorrow the rate his life was headed. A series
of calculated situations, each one more troubling than the
one before it and possibly the one after it, sucked the
marrow from his bones. His wrist looked like he'd
jammed it inside a radiator, one side of his face was puff-
ier than the other, and he'd bit down on his tongue. He
was ready to even the score, but the damn dog wasn't going to do him any favors.

In fact, he discovered one nightmare followed by another, and his throbbing cheek hadn't made it any easier
to sleep. He'd taken drugs—some over-the-counter medication—but that hadn't solved his problem. If he hadn't
been scared of doctors and needles and STDs, he might
have visited the man in the white lab coat with the UNM
medical degree.

Yeah, his world was fucked up, but he was about to
change it with a dog and a needle and the semblance of a
plan.

A damn dog. His life had come down to injecting
man's best friend. And it was all because Harrison Bar-

rymore was a sonofabitch. It had all gone to shit when he pissed his hand away to the girl, and now he needed to do the deed, or he'd end up with a piece of wire wrapped around his neck.

His car barely started and belched oil every five miles or so, and a leaky faucet in his basement apartment that the landlord hadn't bothered to fix, and he'd jammed a toe against his worn-out sofa, and Gwendoline Pearce wanted to toss a fistful of dirt atop his grave.

Hope glistened off Johnny's forehead and found its way to a sea of Escalades and promenades and stucco facades jammed along Central Avenue. His big grin was filled with sin, and he had a needle stuffed in his outer pocket.

The past kicked him in the ass and spit him back out. He'd pounded his head against the wall, he'd pushed his way toward trouble and back again, he'd dealt with conflicting emotions and conflicting dreams, and he'd nearly conquered them all. He'd gotten rid of one bastard, and he owed money to another. He'd bet on cards and horses, and the ponies and dogs, and sports teams, and a sea of pipe dreams, and a plastic ball bouncing around a wheel.

He parked near the back of the lot, around what little shade he could find, and emerged from a vehicle filled with heat into more of the same, where gravel mixed around his feet and sprouts of grass had been devoured by the sun. He downed the last of his water bottle, which dropped his core temperature about two degrees, and tossed it in the nearest trash receptacle. He shoved a wide-brimmed hat onto the top of his small head and weaved his way through the already rowdy crowd.

The throng hopped up and down in their seats, spittle flying from their lips, their words cursing the sky and his broad shoulders. Beer cans and bottles were being tossed underneath metal bleachers, passion and precision meeting him in the front seat and chipping away at his dreams. Loud voices resounded over outstretched speakers, as a sea of jeans and T-shirts and hats stood in rapt attention to the festivities taking place below.

He still remembered the last remnants of a goodbye kiss that lingered on his lips from a lass in a bright pink hat.

The fix was in. That's what he told himself, and even he had trouble believing that particular line of bullshit. It was filled with holes and pores and embers that had escalated his pain and suffering. Had he been smarter, he would have downed an array of blue pills with some red and yellow ones. Or he could have punched a rodeo clown who had frowned in his presence.

He recalled a line Gwendoline had delivered more than once in his presence. "You really are a bastard."

Truer words had never been spoken.

CHAPTER 7

The damn dog licked his hand. The dog had this innocent-looking expression on his face, his head tilted to one side and his tail tilted toward the other. He was wiggling his tail back and forth, and he started running around in circles. When that wasn't enough, the dog took peculiar to a whole new level: He rolled onto his back with his legs sticking up in the air. Johnny looked at the dog, looked at the needle, and looked back at the dog again. The needle was long and filled with evil intent.

The dog was beautiful. Hadn't even barked once, and hadn't looked at him with anything other than curiosity, interest, and love. Johnny had his ID in one pocket, and the needle had been in the other. With his hat low on his head and his purposeful stride, the walk to the kennels where the dogs were kept was much easier than he had anticipated. A series of handshakes, and no ID was even required. The owner had stepped away for a sundae—trusting bastard—and had left the dog all by his lonesome. The dog was starved for attention and wanted a few pats on his soft belly. When the petting started, the wiggling and squirming followed suit, with the licking not far behind. His collar said his name was Sam, and his eyes were the color of milk chocolate.

Johnny took a deep breath, took one more look at the dog, stuck the still-full needle back into his pocket, and walked away as a series of voices headed in his direction. Taking the opposite path, he slunk through the bristling horde.

Sure as shit, this is not going to end well.

e⁄ʒe⁄ʒ

The stands were filled to the brim with women in hats and women without, men in polyester suits and jeans and haunted expressions, other men with tickets waving in the breeze and bouncing around with energy just as intense as that damn dog. Greed and luck permeated throughout the metallic stands, and there were even a few children scattered throughout the gambling playground, standing and dancing atop the metallic benches.

Johnny found a seat in the middle of a half-empty

row and painted a serious expression on his face. With the brim of his hat pulled low, he clasped his hands in front of him, and closed his eyes, praying for some miracle that didn't involve a gunfight and a battering ram, not necessarily in that order.

He could have made a run for it against the tide of unfamiliar faces or waited it out in the bathroom stall while the dogs pranced around the dirt track, or shoved a snub-nosed revolver in his back pocket. Instead, he chose the inconspicuous look and figured a lack of eye contact, along with a heartfelt prayer, would save his sorry ass.

But on this day, his prayer would go unanswered.

The race started, and his heart nearly stopped. Around the first bend, the favorite—the dog he was supposed to inject—was in fourth place and gaining momentum. Around the next bend, things ratcheted in the wrong direction, and Sam moved into second place. He was still in second when the dogs hit the home stretch, and that beautiful little bastard found another gear, his nose poking at the air, snout out, and pushing himself into the lead.

A standing ovation ensued, followed by a glance in his direction from a man in a black polyester suit and even darker sunglasses, and Johnny decided he needed a better exit strategy. Stocky men stood and formed a circle in the crowd, moving slower than his tall, lanky frame, so like that damn dog, his legs started churning against the growing tide, and thoughts of survival, instead of hormone-filled needles, filled the void. His hands and ears rang, a plane cut through the air above, and a church bell resounded in his head. The hands of time stopped for an instant, and so did his feet. Stands clicked and clacked around him, male and female voices cut through the pack, shoving and bumping ensued, and Johnny leaped from one level to the next, bounding down to the ground. Change jingled in his pocket, an elbow caught his right kidney, and his long legs kicked out.

The needle had been tossed into the nearest trash bin. Otherwise, it would have stabbed him on at least three different occasions, and he'd find himself at the end of a short rope, dangling from the tallest tree near the Rio Grande, his bare ass blowing in the breeze. That's how Mark had been strung up, bare-ass naked when he couldn't pay off his debt, and the photos had been sent to his grieving wife, responsible for the care and feeding of their three children. She had hung herself three weeks later.

Johnny barreled through the crowd with his hands in front of his face, his elbows at his sides, as he pushed through bodies left and right. Yelling and cursing belched from shocked faces, as a growing strength formed in his mind, and the instinct for survival took over his every desire. The search for him had ended even before it had begun.

Intensity flowed through his veins, both wonderful and traumatic at the same time. Fury wasn't far behind, as he pushed himself even more. Leaping to the concrete, he pumped his arms, and his legs followed suit, churning faster than a battering ram.

He plowed into a man the size of a refrigerator and dropped to the ground.

"What the hell do you think you're doing?" the man asked.

When Johnny didn't reply, the man pulled his hand back and shoved his fist against Johnny's chin. Johnny's head jerked back and slammed once more against the concrete. He saw stars and stripes and a blinding white light. The picture in his mind turned hazy and unfocused.

The man walked on as Johnny pushed himself to his feet. When he stood, his knees gave out, and his mind gave way, and yet adrenalin allowed him to continue on. He forced a smile, and the pain against his side was real. His jaw tightened, and he snagged a tooth against his lower lip, drawing blood toward his chin. He tested his wrist, flipping it one way and then the other, the crowd parted as three men charged, and he flipped his mind forward. He careened off the concrete wall, the pain in his right shoulder equaled to the one in his side. He tumbled into a woman in high heels: This time she went down, but he didn't. She yelled after him, but he couldn't decipher the words or the accent.

Voices called behind him, and feet slapped around him. Pounding ensued behind him, and maybe a bit of it was even in his head. The pounding resonated in his brain, and he bobbed his head up and down. The voice in his head clanged against steel, the metal bucking and swaying in the breeze. Images filtered through his mind, most of which were discovered during a happier time. His breathing was shallow, hiccupping at the back of his throat, and an arm snagged his shoulder, wrenching him back. Johnny shoved out an elbow, and a sigh formed an inadequate response. His shoulder burned where nails had hit home.

Quarters and nickels and dimes jangled in his pocket, bouncing against one another. His shins screamed, and so did his ankles. A kid yelled above the masses, and Johnny's mouth was filled with a metallic tint.

That damn dog. Johnny should have just done what he was told. But he and easy had parted ways some time ago. If anything, he preferred the series of fireworks that painted the New Mexican skyline.

His hands managed to find trouble on multiple occasions. If he had found a way to quit dialing the phone, quit tossing cards into the center table, and quit tossing his life out of an open window, he might have found a way out of his present predicament.

His existence was futile. He couldn't even inject a dog without backing down from the challenge. Sam's expression was the last thought that entered his mind one final time before his feet struck the gravel of the lot, and he plowed ahead through the divergent crowd. If he wasn't careful, the game would place a paper bag over his head and beat him with a metal wand.

His wheels spun gravel in all directions, as he peeled out of the lot with a nondescript car less than three hundred feet away.

☙❧☙

Gwendoline had met her share of bastards. Even managed to date a few of them and married one for fun. A string of six or seven followed in quick succession. And Johnny was the biggest shitheel of them all. He'd ripped her heart out and fed it to the sharks. He had a smile that was bigger than he was, this aw-shucks attitude that made her weak in the knees, and he'd turned her around and fucked her in the ass. Not literally. But close enough.

She'd swallowed her pride along with more than a little of her breakfast, and then she swallowed it again. He'd practically left her for dead, when he'd walked away, and now he wanted back in her life again. She was ready to kick him in the balls. One swift kick was easier than dealing with the alternative, when she'd been forced to pick up the pieces of her miserable existence. But she wasn't sure she could silence the voices in her head. The demons that had taken over her world pounded her on the head and damn near left her for dead.

Gwendoline had danced in her younger days. Not the dancing that involved poles, but the dancing that involved perfect posture and pointed toes, drifting across a hardwood floor, commanding the attention of a crowded room, her long dress billowing around her, the man with the strong hands clutching her waist and leading her off toward another sunset. And then even that shit stopped working, and her mind stopped filling in the blanks, and the voices in her head slipped, and the rain hadn't been able to wash the pain away.

It had failed miserably.

She had failed miserably.

No, it was more like the bastard had failed. It was easier to blame the shitheel with the grin that could cut through a crowded room. The grin that superseded all other grins and left her feeling bigger than she ever thought possible, ready to take charge with a firm hand and a magic wand. A need. A growing desire to become one with the universe, as she tried to maintain an existence that would allow her to live her life just one more day.

She couldn't get Johnny out of her head. It wasn't that he had hurt her. No, it's that he had taken everything from her, and now he had shown up in her life once more when she was ready to live without him for the rest of her days. That's what made this situation most troubling of all: She was forced to deal with feelings she hadn't felt in years and situations that placed her heart in the middle of a cold, metal table. A cold, metal cocoon in a room filled with padded walls and pills in small plastic cups.

Gwendoline wasn't ready for the stuffing and the gravy, and she wasn't ready for the warm apple pie. But one way or another she would fight her way to the bitter end, or she would find herself clinging to the edge of a cliff, and ready to take the plunge toward the water below.

Worst of all, though, Johnny had given her hope for a better tomorrow.

CHAPTER 8

Johnny punched the accelerator, swerved around a Toyota Tundra, and barreled through a succession of red lights on a main stretch of road. Horns honked and tempers flared, including his own, and, still, the man in the nondescript car lingered in his rearview. He stabbed the radio, turned the music up louder, and clipped a minivan. It spun into a Mercedes, and both vehicles slammed against the curb.

Steam shot up from both cars. Doors were opened, and gestures were made, and, still, his mind shot forward, along with his tires. He flicked his eyes to the passenger seat where only emptiness remained.

He whipped the wheel hard to the left, shot through an alleyway as pedestrians and dogs dove out of the way. His right tire clipped a cart, and bags and clothes dropped around the passenger side. A man in ragged clothes gave him the finger in his rearview mirror.

With the mountains to the east, Johnny headed north, and the car behind him followed suit. He made a hard left on Paseo del Norte, and headed west toward the volcanoes. Traffic congregated around him, and he whipped around cars and trucks and SUVs. He passed a series of modern strip malls with sand-colored stucco siding and pointed roofs. A light turned green, and he barreled through. When the car behind him followed suit, an SUV ran the red and clipped the back end. Johnny allowed himself the faintest hint of a smile, as he continued on underneath a clear blue sky.

❡❡❡

Her location hadn't changed. Gwendoline still lived on the same street in the same home where she had broken it off from him before. Before the downward spiral, hitting rock bottom on the casino floor, and then managing to go even lower.

His mind drifted to the girl and the Indian and the man with the Rolex on his wrist. Johnny still believed that he could come back from the brink of despair and find a happier place with golden sunsets and lizards that stood out from the colors of the sand.

He had checked his rearview mirror countless times,

and each time the nondescript car was gone. He pulled around the corner to the curve at the end, parked his car in the middle of the curvature, and exited the vehicle with one hand in his pocket and the other on the key fob. One single honk, and he was done.

Large stones curved around the lawn in the general direction of the porch, and long strides allowed him to circumnavigate the path with ease. Before he reached the last one, the front door opened, and Gwendoline stared at him with an unforgiving nature. She had one hand on her hip, and her other paw was wrapped around a double-barreled shotgun pointed at a spot on his forehead. The gun did most of the talking.

Johnny placed his hands in the air and took a step closer. "Will you help me?"

She cocked both barrels at the same time. "I don't even like you."

"I have nowhere else to go," he said, "so if you're going to kill me, you might as well get it over with."

Her shoulder flinched, and so did the gun.

"Well, I'm glad we got that settled."

"We haven't settled anything," Gwendoline said. "Once an asshole, always an asshole."

"Is that the best you've got?"

She poked him in the chest with both barrels. "You're about to feel a world of pain."

"I'm sure it can't be any worse than what I've felt

the last two years of my life. Maybe if I had kept drinking—"

Her eyes dropped to the gun and then stared hard
through the New Mexican sun. "I don't care. You're out
of my life."

"I never stopped loving you."

She flinched, and nearly dropped the gun. "You're
full of shit."

A crack formed in her façade, and he leaned in to
touch her upper arm. He stroked her bicep and wrapped a
strand of hair behind her left ear. The gun dug into a spot
near his heart, but he didn't push it out of the way. "It's
all I know."

"It's been two years, you bastard," she replied. "And
I just lost my job."

"Maybe we can help each other."

The gun pressed forward. "Stalk much?"

He had followed her, learned all he could about her,
and had never forgotten her, despite her mad rush for the
front door in the middle of the night after he came home
with a black eye and a busted chin. He didn't have the
heart to tell her what happened, but Gwendoline had
known just the same, and she managed to walk out on
him without a solitary goodbye. Her back had always
packed more punch than her front, and the nagging feeling at the back of his mind had hurt him worse than she
ever could. He concentrated on his mistakes, not his suc-

cesses, and she had been his biggest mistake. No matter how much he wanted to, he could never let her go.

Johnny's eyes hardened. "I don't have to admit it to you."

She laid the shotgun on the floor and opened the door. Her floor was as clean and unencumbered as she was, and her nails were long and pink. Her hair was straight and framed her face, and her pants were rolled at the cuffs.

Gwendoline rolled her eyes. "We're going to have to discuss a few details."

Johnny lifted an eyebrow. "Is that the start of a plan?"

"It's the start of something all right," she said. "But it doesn't mean you're any less of a bastard."

He stepped inside and closed the door. With her hands on her hips, she blocked his way forward and informed him not to come any closer, or she might use her gun. He blinked first and shrugged, and this led to a firm hand against his face. This time he didn't blink or change his expression. Instead, he stood up taller.

He shifted his stance. "Do you even want to know what I've gotten myself in the middle of now?"

She placed her palm flat against his chest, adding the additional physical barrier to the mental one. "Probably not."

"But you want to ask me anyway."

She shook her head, but her hand remained. The contact seared through his clothes, and nearly burned his skin.

He kept his eyes focused on her lips, but her frown remained firmly in place. The standoff lasted for a minute, and he was convinced he might need to make the first move. He didn't.

"Do you like being an asshole?"

Not exactly. "Always." It was the answer she would have expected from him, and he didn't want to disappoint her again.

"You on the path to improvement?" she asked.

"I'm headed down that road, but I took a left when I should have made a right."

She eyed him suspiciously. "And that's how you ended up here?"

The narrow hallway closed in tighter, and his thoughts constricted. "Even if it were true, you wouldn't believe me. You'd tell me I did it on purpose."

She narrowed her eyes. "What?"

"Gambling."

"It's more than a convenient problem," Gwendoline said. "It's an addiction. Until you admit as much, you won't be able to help yourself."

"I can win, you know. The losing…it won't last forever."

"Isn't that how you ended up in this mess in the first

place?" She peered at him with harsh eyes. "You're a rather curious individual."

The silence lasted more than a minute before she motioned him toward the living room. He didn't stop her. Her behind moved in a rather elegant fashion, and the faintest hint of a smile formed on his lips.

"One foot in front of the other," he said.

"Stop staring at my ass." She stopped midstride, looked over her shoulder, and started up again. The hem of her pants danced across the floor. "Or something like that."

Her temper always spoke louder than the rest of her, and her eyes grew wider with the passage of time. She took up residence on the sofa and told him to stand with his hands behind his back. Since she was the one with the gun, he obliged her.

The gun, while it currently rested at her feet, was not far out of her reach.

He opened his mouth, thought better of it, and closed it.

She shifted her position on the microfiber. "Don't try to be cute."

"I'd rather be cute than dead," he said.

She rubbed the arm of the sofa and pulled her hands in close to her chest. "Is that what you're up against?"

"I have no idea."

Her eyes blazed. "Surely, you have some clue."

"I probably do," he said. *But telling her wouldn't further my cause or hers.*

Gwendoline slapped the arm of the sofa and glared at him. "But you're not going to tell me?"

"And hurt you all over again?"

She rubbed the left side of her face. "You had no problem doing it before."

"Doesn't mean I enjoyed it." But Johnny did enjoy the pleasure of her company more than he should. The thought of her made his current tribulations worth it in the end.

"Well, at least you haven't resorted to being a total shitheel."

He did have his moments. "I did love you."

She waved him off. "Don't feed me another line. I'm too old for that shit."

"No, you're not." His voice softened. "But you're jaded." After all, she had been the one to walk away.

"Are you trying to psychoanalyze me now?"

He scratched his forearm. "If that's what it takes—"

"For what?"

"To get you back into my life again."

She shook her head. "Don't feed me another line. You just want my help."

"So what if I do?" he asked. "Is that so wrong?"

She sank deeper into the maroon and gray sofa. "Depends on what you're offering in return."

"My heart."

Gwendoline glared at him and popped up from her cocoon. "Now, I know you're full of shit."

"Oh, I'm full of something all right."

"You're full of a lot of things," she said, "but that doesn't mean I have to believe a single one of them."

                   co&co

Gwendoline had a sanctuary. A safe house. But she wasn't about to drop him in the middle of it and let him wiggle his way out. It would have been easier that way. Minus the wiggling. The jiggling was also another loose end that she'd somehow have to tie up herself. Then she'd find herself up against some immovable object and picking daisies out of her rear end. And she'd find herself somehow losing all over again. She'd always been good at that sort of thing, picking the losers out of a lineup. Even if there were only two out of ten, she'd manage to find the two, and then do it all over again.

Gwendoline had more than a few challenges come her way. And she'd curse the heavens and swear at the universe, and punch the wall. Plaster rained down around her, ears ringing at the uncompromising sound, and her feet pounded against the ground. The carpet moved with her feet, and her shoulders hunched in some haphazard manner. Her ears rang, and her lips moved, but no sound came out. Johnny was a glorified bastard, but she couldn't erase her memory and their history.

The voices in her head called her and shouted out around her. The sound of the rain slapped down, and the wind whistled through the open window. Her hands covered her ears, and yet there was still sound that managed to work its way through.

She had the bastard with the winning smile and the false impression. A man who needed no additional explanation and who challenged her without really pushing her at all. He made her feel incomplete and somehow worthless, and yet she still craved more. What did that say about her? She was more than a little inclined to fill in a few of the details.

The road was filled with dips and dives, and more than a few potholes, and she was more than adept to seek out the challenges, and let the pressure lead her. Her heart, after all, had failed her long ago.

ೞೞೞ

Gwendoline picked up a pillow and hugged it to her chest. "Do you even know what you're running from?"

He wasn't really sure that he did. Only that he needed to continue down the same path, otherwise he was going to find himself at the short end of a long rope, and he was going to be left holding more than a few pieces up to the sun. He had lost a few dreams along the way and scattered the ashes around the playground. He wasn't sure he could live with the consequences or much of anything for that matter. But he did have a hold on the future, or at least the past.

Johnny had passed out somewhere along the way, only to be revived again, and then he was back in the forefront with a thought or two in his head, and he dreamed one dream right after another, counting his demons along with his charms. He had filled his head with one thought and then another, marching back and forth in the road together, picking his feet up when he was about to hit the floor, and filling his head with more than a few memories. He had one road filled with passion and one road filled with heartache, and he wasn't really sure which one would end up ahead.

The game had only just started, and the shotgun was still poised close to her person.

A look of abject horror swept across Johnny's face as he tried to get past some strange place where the sea was wide, and the water was shallow, and where his thoughts danced with those from tomorrow. He couldn't handle the thought of loss.

The air shifted around him, and he bounced on the balls of his feet. Her hand glided in front of her face, and her expression had a tinge of whimsicalness.

He didn't have the heart to push through, to shove

her brick wall aside, but he did have the desire. He did have his thoughts jumbled together, one piling on top of another. It probably shouldn't have been that way, but there wasn't a thing he could do about it. If he could have extracted her from his head, he would have, but it wasn't that easy.

Instead, his mind refocused on his present predicament, and he walked toward the front door. Gwendoline didn't call after him.

✌⊃✌⊃

Johnny stood in front of the infernal contraption, his eyes blazing, his thoughts convoluted and jumbled as his mind swam with an infinite number of possibilities. With his cash situation on permanent deflation, he needed a few more dollars to stuff in his pants. His voice caught in the back of his throat. There was no one around. Darkness gathered around him and wrapped him in a cloak. His hair was still wet from the shower he had taken, and the back of his head was aching. His home with the pitched roof and the stucco siding was just down the street, at the back end of a cul-de-sac. The blackened street was otherwise silent around him, and beats of rain tapped him on the shoulder.

Light illuminated the apparatus, and an overhead light just out of his reach made him blink more than once.

The sound of shoes tapped the sidewalk, bringing him back to reality, and once more the machine flickered in his direction. He punched the keys and waited. The machine blinked again, and he tapped another key. The machine clicked and clacked, and a multitude of bills belched out. He gathered them up in the palm of his hand, the square edges sticking out in either direction, and shuffled through them with his thumb and index finger, before stuffing them in his pocket and turning around.

"Where do you think you're going, buddy?" the man said. He wore an overcoat, a sour expression, dark sunglasses, and a beard that covered half his face. His hands were the size of hams, and he cracked his knuckles underneath the flickering light.

"Away from here."

The voice deepened. "Not with that amount of money you're not."

"Is this a robbery?"

The strange man held out his hand, along with a gun the size of a battering ram. "It's whatever you want to call it."

Johnny smiled and handed over the cash. The man blinked and stuffed the bills into his front pocket. Compassion had left the air long ago, and a gray haze had taken over.

The cracks of light compounded, and night lifted Johnny off his feet. Or it might have been the strange man with the ham-sized hands and the glimmer of a whisper eliciting from his lips.

Johnny knocked the gun away and reached for the mass of bills. The man laughed and mumbled an incoherent phrase with a thick accent. The man's foot struck Johnny's knee, and Johnny tumbled to the ground. Long hair swept across the man's face as Johnny was taken to some other place. A foot came down, and he rolled away. Not far enough, though. A glancing blow blasted his right kidney. Johnny coughed and sighed in response. He gasped for breath, picked himself up, brushed himself off, and leaned a little too far forward.

The next blow caught him on the chin, and Johnny stumbled back once again. He tossed out a couple rights and more than a few lefts and caught only dead air for his trouble. Two kicks went nowhere, and still the bills—and the man—taunted him. A single blow caught its intended target, but the smile on the strange man only grew wider.

Another blow caught Johnny on the chin, and he spit a glob of blood onto the concrete. One kick jammed the man in the crotch, and a dull roar filled the otherwise dead space. Rain licked Johnny's face and dribbled down his chin, and he slogged through the heavy air around him. A roundhouse smacked the left side of his face, and he smacked the pavement with a thud.

This time, he didn't get back up.

When Johnny did wake up, the rest of his money was

gone, but his wallet remained. It was morning. The sun nearly blinded him, and he shivered from the cold and the rain of the evening before. His pants were dirty, and so was he. His voice shook, and so did his hands. The sound of a distant horn managed to fill the void, and a siren overtook the horns and the traffic.

The blanks in his head were crowded, the gaps as wide as the desert sand. He stood up, slapped the dirt on his pants, and spit on the ground underneath his feet.

When he slid his ATM card into the slot once more, the machine beeped and clicked and spit his card back out again. He cursed under his breath, tried again, and received the same result. The asshole had cleaned him out.

The gun in his pocket was gone. During the blitz attack, he hadn't even thought to pull it out, and now it was probably at the bottom of the Rio Grande or tossed in a dumpster a mile away, or maybe it was used in some random shooting on some random street by a thug that was wanted in Arizona.

Placing his hands over his ears, he took off running and tripped on a crack in the broken sidewalk. He was grinning from ear to ear as he executed a perfect face plant. He wiped his cheek and flicked blood from his fingertips.

CHAPTER 9

Johnny banged on the door with his left hand before he slipped through the threshold. A calm voice reverberated in his head, but he shoved it back down. The voice of reason had taken a vacation, and insanity had risen to the challenge. He had a few coins and a few pieces of lint in his pocket, and a woman named Gwendoline who wanted little to do with him. He had walked out on her, or she had walked out on him. Either way, it didn't matter. His stolen wad didn't matter.

The bank was empty, or nearly so. There were two people in line ahead of him, and there were two tellers waiting on three customers. The daughter held her mother's hand and looked into her eyes, before glancing over her right shoulder. The grin gripped her face from ear to ear. He offered a tentative smile in return.

He stood at the back of the line going over and over the plan in his mind. The simplicity of it. The sheer boldness. The cloud of sadness had set in and rained down from the sky above with a harsh wind added to the mix. The voices in his head called him, and motivation slammed against his forehead. His legs jittered and jabbered, knocking against each other. He breathed in deep and let it back out. His head pounded, and his right knee ached from a sports injury two years ago. He stared at the little girl with the braids in her hair for longer than he should have, and then his eyes flicked to the teller with the dark skin and perfect hair.

He looked at his left wrist, where his watch should have been, and shifted his head from side to side. He tapped his jacket where the gun had been stuffed in his pocket. He counted backward from ten, swallowed down the last of his pride, extracted the gun from his pocket— one of those back alley deals less than fifteen minutes ago—and executed his plan.

"Nobody move." Johnny fired a bullet at a random ceiling tile. "Put your hands in the air."

"Which do you want us to do?" a timid voice asked. The man looked as though he might tip over at any moment.

"Oh my God, he has a gun," the mother said.

The little girl stared at him with wide eyes and opened her mouth, but no sound came out.

Time slowed down, and the air grew heavy with fear. At least part of it was his own, but he shoved it back down and took three steps forward. The lobby was cold and hard and big. With each step, his shoes squeaked across the tan tile.

"This is a holdup," Johnny said. "I want all the cash from your drawers. The rest of you lay face down on the ground."

"Is that your plan?" The lines on the mother's face were harsh and even. Her three-inch heels made her seem like a monster.

The little girl gripped her hand tighter and shuffled in place.

"This is not a negotiation," Johnny said. The gun rifled through the air. "Hand over your BlackBerries."

"Are you looking to cause trouble?" the timid voice asked. It had a slight squeak.

"I'm looking for cash." He fired another shot at the same ceiling tile. Dust rained down from above. "Face down on the ground. I will not ask you again."

The little girl glared at him, her eyes and gaze intense. The smile was gone, and it was replaced with a look of pure hatred. She gripped her mother's hand tighter and dropped to the ground.

Her mother offered up an older version of the same look. "You're not going to get away with this."

He didn't offer up a reply. Instead, he grabbed the

bag from the male teller and marched out the front door, his stride elongated for the momentous occasion, before he took off down the street.

He flipped his hood up, and the breeze batted at the fabric. Dropping his head, Johnny quickened his pace, shortened his strides, and took the pressure away from the rest of his body. A chill came over him, and a bout of shivering soon followed. The shot of adrenaline nearly overwhelmed him, as he stumbled forward against the breeze. His hand covered his mouth and then drifted to the left side of his face.

He had a wide smile, and a bag of money dangled at his waist.

The entire scene had happened in less than three minutes.

⋐⋗⋐⋗

Three hours later, Johnny had a motel room on the opposite end of town. A black Cadillac had taken up residence outside his abode and had stuck around through last night and this morning. The streetlamp overhead had been shattered before he entered his room. The money in the bag was less than he had hoped, and he knew he needed more. Otherwise, he couldn't execute the last part of his plan.

He had little money, and even fewer options, and a

bruise that covered the left side of his face. He had broken dreams, a sore jaw, and a headache that he couldn't seem to fix with Tylenol. He had a bank breathing over his shoulder, so he decided to rob the same bank that had denied his most recent loan request. The tellers and customers were collateral damage, but it was a situation he couldn't seem to avoid.

The motel had bars on the windows, gravel in the lot, and a group with guns across the street. He paid in cash and offered up no identification. The manager hadn't even looked at him twice. He handed Johnny an old-fashioned key before he turned his head away and focused on the twenty-inch TV.

Johnny had lost the tail at a red light about a mile from his present location, and his room was on the second floor, facing the parking lot. He had already witnessed one verbal altercation, and the couple out front appeared to be gearing up for round two. He couldn't decide which woman was worse.

After he had a nap and a drink from the liquor store two doors down, he counted his money. The results were disconcerting.

He punched the dresser, and it wobbled in response, but otherwise remained silent. He stomped his feet and grabbed another drink from the red bottle. It tickled the back of his throat, as it eased its way down, and the anger momentarily subsided. He flipped on the TV and saw his face on the screen. His head jerked, and he stumbled back against the bed.

When calmness entered his universe, he took one final drink, tossed the bottle in the trash, and trudged outside. He slammed the door, circumnavigated the stairs, and bumped the two women with the front of his body.

Neither offered a response, as he continued on his way.

He turned his key in the ignition, and his car hiccupped before coming to life. Gravel kicked up in all directions as he pulled out of the parking lot.

The convenience store was less than three miles away.

"What the hell do you want?" the clerk asked.

Johnny's mood was grim. "I want your money."

He had come inside only moments ago. Aside from a clerk with a newspaper on his left side and a crossword puzzle on his right, the store was empty. The aisles were jammed with candy bars, hygiene items, and windshield-washer fluid.

Several freezers lined the back of the store, and a strong odor of cigarette smoke and throw up came from the right. Two of the lights flickered overhead at a regular rate.

The clerk narrowed his eyes. "You look a little strung out."

Johnny plopped a red bottle on the counter with one

hand and withdrew his gun with the other. "I've had a lot to drink."

At the sight of the gun, the clerk showed no sign of fear, but he did show more than a hint of curiosity. His voice, though, rose an octave in response. "And you want more?" The pen in the clerk's right hand shook before he covered his right hand with his left. "What are you going to do with that bottle?"

Johnny gritted his teeth. "I'm going to bust it over your head if you don't give me what I want."

Behind the counter, the clerk shifted on his feet, and his hair flopped down into his eyes. "What's with the cut?" he asked. "And the bruises?"

"It's been a long day."

The clerk nodded his head in reply. "I'm sure it has been."

"And it's about to get even longer without a compromise—"

The clerk's eyes shifted. "What?"

"The cash drawer," Johnny said.

The clerk leaned backward. "Now?"

Johnny picked up the bottle and dropped it on the counter. The gun remained steady in his other hand. "I'm not going to wait forever."

The smile on Johnny's face was genuine, but the rest of him wasn't. The rest of him was ready to migrate east for the winter. Maybe then he wouldn't have a chill rocketing through his body, and a clerk with long hair and a cold stare offering up a blank face in response. Maybe then the light would calm down along with his mind. Maybe he wouldn't have to worry about the remaining bills in his bag. And maybe he wouldn't have to worry about an ex who had given him the cold shoulder.

The clerk reached into the cash drawer and pulled out a thick wad. He handed the cash across the laminate countertop with a halfhearted smile and pulled out a shotgun. When the clerk cocked the hammer, that was right about the time Johnny served up a bullet right between the clerk's eyebrows.

The man with the long hair dropped to the ground, twitched once, and was no more.

Johnny leaned over the laminate; grabbed the rest of the cash that had fallen to the floor, a pack of cigarettes, and a lighter; and took off at a dead run. He had the bottle of scotch to keep him company during the night and coming days, and once the bottle was gone, he would have nothing at all.

He had forecasted trouble, and he had met the concern head-on without a single hint of underestimation, even though he would have preferred to do a few more calculations in his head. The clerk, though, managed to calculate incorrectly and bled out for his trouble.

He had walked in and out in less than five minutes, and those were five minutes he could never get back.

❦❦❦

The street was crowded, and so was his mind. One thought slipped away, and another took its place. One dream had crowded Johnny's mind, and another had clouded his judgment. He had one belief that he couldn't quite hold onto, and he had another right before the sidewalk met his knee. The slightest hint of compassion lingered in his mind. He couldn't shake the feeling that had taken over his brain, as his simple plan had turned out much more complicated. His life had taken a turn for the worse. He had the will and the way, and neither had managed to be with him today.

A baby carriage blocked his path, and when he sidestepped around it, a blonde was in his way. She fell to the ground, and so did he. She glared at him, and then her foot shot out. The next thing he knew, he was on the ground again and clutching below his waist. The pain hummed and throbbed, and his mind shut down to keep the darkness at bay. The voice in his head resounded louder, pressure mounted, and pain took over his world. He writhed on the ground, wiggling back and forth, his face red, his eyes dark.

His mind was clamped in a cage. The lights had nearly gone out, and his eyes watered. He opened his mouth, but no sound came out.

The blonde walked on.

ɛ⁄ɔɛ⁄ɔ

The Albanian didn't refer to himself as a hit man. He provided a particular service for a particular group of people who managed to pay him large sums of money for his trouble. He had a client list that filled a single black book, and he picked his jobs with care and ease. He took pride in his work and had never botched a job.

His hair was pulled back in a ponytail, and gray plastered the majority of his outfit. His two dimples and perfect teeth made ladies swoon, and flexing his biceps had ruptured more than one T-shirt. He had a nondescript car for this nondescript job.

The entire length of the call was less than forty-six seconds. A picture, address, and details of the job were emailed to his cell phone less than three minutes later.

He stopped his dinner with the former model who had decided Albuquerque was the perfect place to hide, dropped a wad of bills on the white tablecloth, kissed his date for the evening on her left cheek, and exited the restaurant, abandoning a half-eaten meal and somewhat promising conversation.

He took his jacket from the attendant just inside the door, grabbed the change of clothes hanging in the backseat, stepped into the men's room, and locked the door behind him.

Five minutes later, he emerged a brand-new man

with his former clothes on the hangar, and a ball cap pulled down over his eyes.

His car was sleek and muscular like him, and he gunned the engine hard as he merged onto the busy street. Seven guns, two knives, multiple boxes of ammunition, night vision goggles, and a single sword filled his trunk, with most of his weapons placed in a dark canvas bag. He had a .44 Magnum jammed in his glove compartment for emergency purposes. The weapon had only been fired on one previous occasion, but it had saved his life.

He kept his speed just under the limit and stopped at every yellow light, much to the chagrin of multiple drivers, two of which offered up the middle finger. On both occasions, The Albanian smiled, shook his head, and shrugged in the rearview mirror.

Classical music emitted from the car's speakers, and he nodded his head along to the music. His mind lit up at the violin crescendo, and his foot eased down on the brake. The three volcanoes appeared on the horizon, and with his window down, the New Mexican rain offered up a familiar odor as his left elbow rested on the seam.

When he arrived at his destination, he popped the trunk and stuffed three guns and one knife in various locations. He tossed the cap in the trunk before he slammed the lid.

The Albanian approached her door with a whistle and a grin.

℮ↄℯↄ

The man on the other side of the door was unfamiliar to her. His face was chiseled, and his skin was tan, and his smile seemed genuine. His outfit was dark and had been pressed recently. His hair was tied in the back, and he waved his hands—there were only four fingers on his left—in front of the door. He stood at a slight angle, his stance slightly off-balance.

He peered at his clipboard. "I have a delivery for Gwendoline Pearce."

"Who the hell are you?"

"Just the delivery guy. Nothing more."

"Leave it next to the door," Gwendoline said.

"Sorry, you have to sign for it."

She contemplated the man, his cheesy grin, the clipboard in his right hand, and his tanned skin. In the end, her curiosity won. "What is it?"

"I don't actually open the packages, ma'am. I just deliver 'em."

Not the first time she'd heard that line. "Don't call me ma'am."

He glanced down at his wrist. "Are you going to open the door, or should I come back in the morning?"

She walked to the window, pulled back the curtain, and stared at a sea of familiar vehicles. "Where's your van?"

"I parked it on the next street over," he said. "I need-ed the exercise."

Yeah, right. "You don't look like any UPS driver I've ever met, and you certainly don't work for the postal service."

"We're a high-end delivery service focusing on spe-cialty items."

The box did catch her attention. It sat at his feet.

"You're wearing a black outfit."

His grin widened. "Did I mention we're high end?"

"You have an accent and a scar across your chin."

ⲉⲛⲟⲉⲛⲟ

He held the package up to the peephole and shook it. Then he stepped back and shifted his posture to the other side.

The door opened a crack, and he took another step back. One eye poked through the crack, and the door opened wider.

When the door was opened all the way, The Albani-an made his move. He tossed the package—it was filled with Styrofoam and pebbles—into the nearest bush and clocked his prey on the chin. She stumbled backward and covered her face with both hands. She kicked out at him with her bare feet and caught him on the upper thigh. Nothing more.

He jabbed her in the stomach with his left hand. A puff of air escaped from between her lips. The sigh pitched higher when he punched her between the tits, catching her breastbone. She tilted back and then forward, and he caught her with a perfectly timed uppercut. Her mouth turned slack, and she fell against the door, the back of her skull narrowly missing the wood.

The Albanian stood over her and tilted his head from side to side, loosening the muscles in his tightened neck. While he stared at her face, he felt a foot between his legs. The foot rammed upward again, even harder than it did the first time, and his eyes watered in response. He stepped back as she rolled to her knees and lifted herself to her feet.

Gwendoline's mouth opened, blood dribbled down her chin, and some incoherent response left her lips. A string of curse words followed, and a shit-eating grin filled with blood and spit occupied the quiet.

She tossed a jab in his direction that missed by two feet. While his attention was focused on the ladylike punch, she stepped forward, quicker than a rabbit, and kneed him in the groin.

He bit his lip, his eyes watered harder, and a white light appeared above her head. The air whistled, or maybe that was him. A motorcycle roared to life as a metallic taste formed in his mouth, and he uttered an incoherent response. She kneed him three times in quick succession.

He tipped back and smacked the hardwood with a splat.

While he was on his back, solid bone beat his already sensitive region. Then knees were on his chest, and a series of punches that went on for over a minute nearly split his face in two. And somewhere along the way, he lost consciousness. His final thought before he slipped under was the fact that he had been outsmarted by a shoeless female with long dark hair and an awful grin.

The Albanian's life was seriously fucked up.

ᘓᘎᘓᘎ

Gwendoline's stomach quivered, and both her breasts were on fire. Her mouth was filled with blood and acid, and she had to bite down on her upchuck reflex. Her knees ached, her breath came in short spurts, and her world was filled with an explosion of color. She had her hands on her hips and leaned forward. Wiping her mouth with the back of her hand, she swiped her hand on her workout pants.

The man below her was bigger and much less awkward than she had expected. He also lacked a wallet, or identification of any kind. His breathing was shallow, and his heartbeat slowed, but he was still very much alive. He had blood on his face from where her ring had opened a cut, and he had a stupid expression around the blood.

Gwendoline turned him to the side and poked

through the remainder of his pockets. She found half a pack of chewing gum, a half-filled bottle with some pale-colored pills, and a gun that was twice the size of her hand. She picked it up, pulled back the hammer, assumed the appropriate stance, and pointed it out in front of her at a spot on the wall just above eye level.

Less than a minute later, she stepped forward with one leg on either side of his body, pointed the gun at his forehead, and fired. Both the gun and her hand bucked, she pitched backward about four feet and landed on her backbone, as her whole body convulsed and her lower lip quivered.

ᴄ⌒ᴄ⌒ᴅ

Lapu Sinquah had his man. The bastard was lounging on a park bench at eleven o'clock at night, smoking a cigarette. The ten o'clock news had been Johnny Chapman's downfall. The owner with the in-store camera had notified the proper person—which happened to be Harrison Barrymore—before he contacted the local authorities. The splattered and battered clerk had no idea what happened in his final moments before he left this world for the spirit one.

Johnny might have been a horrible card player, but he was no idiot. Except for the haze of smoke that surrounded his head, he was otherwise coherent and even appeared normal. The light of the moon reflected off of Johnny, and several moments of silence surrounded the nearly empty park. A homeless man shoving a shopping cart through the other end of the park on a set of squeaky, unsteady wheels interrupted the peace.

Lapu wore a neutral expression and a chain around his neck. His outfit was covered in brown and turquoise, and his shoes cushioned his feet. He had an offer on the table, and one in his bank account, and the promise of more money with a confirmed kill.

He lifted his head and stared at the blinking sky before he dropped his gaze to the ground. Each stride was filled with more purpose than the one before it, and each breath he took lingered longer on his lips. The grass had been trampled on recently, and there were remnants from multiple families and picnics, and a Frisbee leaned against the tallest tree.

The man on the bench hadn't moved, nor had he acknowledged Lapu's presence. One cigarette ended, and another took its place. The haze of smoke widened and took on a life of its own.

e/oe/o

The Indian favored his left leg over his right. When he moved, there was a slight delay on his left side. The limp was nearly nonexistent, but Johnny was astute enough to catch it. Despite his observation, his expression didn't change. He also recognized why the Indian was here, and what it meant for the amount of time he had left. The man was no trained assassin, but his reputation preceded him, and he had been tossed out of more than one bar for his trouble.

A biker clad in leather spent multiple days in the hospital and was forced to suck platefuls of red Jell-O with a straw.

When the Indian was close enough, Johnny sighed. "What do you think you're doing?"

The Indian's shoulders shifted. "I'm taking you in."

"Who the hell are you?"

The Indian turned his head to the side and squinted. "The man for the job."

"You're full of shit then," Johnny replied.

"This is bigger than you."

Johnny shook his head. "You really don't think you can win, do you?"

When the Indian made no further comment, Johnny took off running. His feet slapped the pavement, and his arms moved in time to his strides. He veered right into the burnt grass and weaved haphazardly through the small brush.

The Indian stood his ground. "Let me know when you're ready to give up."

Johnny pumped his arms even faster, and his strides

grew longer. His legs were shorter, but he was more than prepared for the chase.

Against the man with the limp, he had a definite advantage, and his mind reached a sense of euphoria.

He turned his head to check on his adversary and bumped his chest against the tree. He stumbled back, the Indian leaped, and the two of them tumbled to the soft ground.

The Indian tossed his fists at Johnny's face, chest, and arms. Johnny rolled from one side to the other, but he caught the brunt of the punches in the desired locations. He bent his knee, lifted upward, and tossed the Indian to the side. Johnny dove on the man and executed a series of lefts and rights. The punches struck bone and cartilage before the Indian heaved Johnny away.

When the Indian reached his feet, he pulled a gun. Johnny batted it away, and it fell to the ground. He executed a perfect kick to the side of the Indian's head, and spittle pitched from the man's lips. He struck the ground, bucked once, and was silent.

Johnny kicked the Indian then did it again, multiple times. He kicked out until he was gasping for breath, and the man seemed to have left this world for the next. Johnny reached down, felt for a pulse on his neck, and discovered none.

But that wasn't the end of Johnny's plan.

CHAPTER 10

Johnny picked his legs up higher, and his arms followed suit. He leaned slightly forward, the wind caressing his back. His eyes darted ahead, seeing the gaps, the holes in traffic. He plowed onward, and a car slammed on its brakes, inches away from his face. A foreign man leaned outside his window and started yelling in a language Johnny didn't understand. The car inched forward, a runner bumped into him, and the pavement came up to meet him. His tailbone throbbed, the light turned green, and more traffic whizzed around him. He staggered to his feet, brushed off his pants, and waited the appropriate amount of time. When the road was clear, he stumbled forward. He swiveled his hips with each movement of his arms and legs, and his joints screamed in protest. He shouted, his voice rising above the wind,

but singing and horn honking was the world's only response.

He tasted sand in his mouth, and a hiccup formed on
his lips. An elbow was tossed in his side by a powerwalk-
ing man with a headband and headphones jammed over
his ears. A flash went off, and Johnny turned his head in
the opposite direction. A door opened, and a man in a
leather jacket stumbled out into the night.

Johnny's leg buckled, a car horn blew, then another
one, and then he was on the other side of the street, and
the smile on his face returned. He made a hard right and
headed for an abandoned parking lot, green with dark
patches and burnt out overhead lights. His breath hitched
in his chest, and he nearly bent over, but somehow his
legs held this time. The wind shifted again, and this time
it slammed into his face instead of his back. His breathing
turned shallow, the cold smacked against his nose, his
cheeks stung, and the mist in his eyes grew. The sounds
around him softened. His knees knocked and locked, and
he stumbled to the ground, catching the pavement in both
his palms.

A woman to his right leaped into the air and slapped
him in the face. He slammed against the concrete. He
twisted, rolled away, and another one jumped on top of
him. And before he knew it there were three women. He
was holding his hands up in the air and being slammed
around, rocking back and forth. The rabbit punches

slammed against his face, neck, and chest. The three women screamed. He bucked one off and then another, picked himself up, and sprinted in the opposite direction.

More yelling followed, and more cursing ensued. A man in a leather jacket staggered after him, and teenagers flooded the street.

Johnny picked up the pace, shifted his head to the left, and his world went from gray to black. He shook his head this way and that, and the fog cleared. The man in the leather jacket grinned, and there was a dark spot where a tooth should have been. The blow was pre-planned, and he delivered it with the utmost precision. Maybe the man was sober, or nearly so. The blow rocked against Johnny's face. He shoved out with his right hand and marched on. The man fell back, but the side of John-ny's face ached.

He passed several storefronts of an indiscriminate nature. The windows were seamless and never-ending. Two were restaurants, one was a consumer electronics store, two others were stacked with clothes, and the last one was a jewelry store where large rubies could be seen through the front window.

His head turned to one side and then the other, his spirit lifted at the sound of rap music blaring through the open window of a pickup. The maze of emotions clouded his judgment, and the pain in his lower back shifted with each step. He bit down on his lip, tasted blood in his mouth, and the pain reminded him of better times. An image formed, and he couldn't shove it down, nor could he shove it away. He lifted his head up high and placed his hand in front of his face, staring at an intricate weave of lines. His mind shifted forward and backward through time, and he filled in the blanks with happier memories.

A single existence formed in his mind, and he blended the moments together, torn from one another, still drifting amongst the black and gray. One sound made him call out, and he screamed at an image of a man with a gun. The pain in his side had shifted to his forehead. Despite his spirit failing him, and the strange women accosting him, and the drunken man who wasn't drunk at all attacking him, Johnny wasn't about to slow down.

☙☙☙

A cab pulled up, and Johnny hopped in the backseat. He'd called for a ride fifteen minutes ago, and the man had been stuck in traffic. The driver had one eye on the dashboard, and one eye in the rearview. The dreadlocks stretched down his face, and his voice was higher than a kite floating in the breeze. The blond hair was dyed, and the face was pockmarked. He had a gold tooth and a slight stutter. His eyes darted in every direction before he blinked and flipped the car into gear.

"Where we headed?" the driver asked.

Johnny rubbed his eyes and his forehead. "Closest bar."

"Looking to develop a few problems?"

"Forget 'em."

The driver shrugged. "Worth a shot."

A lapse in conversation soon followed. Johnny stared out the window, looking at nothing in particular, and searching his mind for a goal or some perspective that might help him entertain a way out of this mess. He had one light shining above him, and the other was slightly more problematic. He had a grin, forced, and he had a situation that he had somehow stepped in the middle of and couldn't see a clear way out. He had hope, lapsed, and a chill had developed in the air through the faulty air conditioner and the cold, starry night. He had a soul, but it had been lost somewhere between the drunk and the three women.

He had a voice. Solid. Powerful. Not as powerful as it could have been, but powerful enough to turn heads and inject fault into the universe. Impactful. It shot through him, and around him.

Colors exploded in his mind, and the high-pitched voice blared near the front of his head. He turned around, looking out the rear window, hoping to see something wonderful.

The words in his head rolled around, and the faces passed before his eyes. And he was sure it was all over, that his world was going to end, and the sky, rich in bright stars and black, would glow for hours.

He hiccupped and slapped a hand over his mouth.

The driver slammed on the brakes and whipped his head around. "Give me all your money."

"What?"

The driver glared and flipped the locks on the doors. "You heard me. I'm not playing games."

"I'm not either."

The light turned green, a horn honked, the car behind whipped into the left lane, and the woman offered up a finger to the stalled cab.

"This is a damn holdup." The driver produced a gun from the glove compartment and a bent smile from his repertoire.

"You're a damn cabbie."

"Not today, pal," the driver said. "Today I'm your worst nightmare. You might want to keep that in mind the next time you get in a cab."

"I will."

The driver cocked back the hammer. "Your money, or your life—it's your call."

Johnny rubbed his face. His side flared up, but he focused on the empty seat and the lack of a crowd around him. His door was locked, and the barrel of the gun was the size of a drum. "Shit, man. Here you go."

He tossed a wad of bills on the passenger seat. The

cabbie flipped the locks, and Johnny opened the door and took off. He was fucking tired of this shit. Flushing his life down the toilet might have been faster, and it might have even improved his present predicament.

❧❧

The world was wrapped around his neck, and it was more than ready to cut off his air supply. Madness. Johnny had a wad of bills in his pocket, much smaller than it was before the robbery, and his shirt had torn on his way out the door. His cheek was bruised, his side was busted, and he favored one leg over the other. He had lost purpose, and more than a little direction, and he was fairly certain he hadn't seen the end of Harrison's goons.

He didn't have much of a plan, but then he'd never needed one before.

His feet pounded through the wind and the rain. He stopped every now and then to put his hand in the air when another clunker went by, but so far his luck was virtually non-existent. He had received one catcall, and one middle finger for his trouble, but otherwise the night was as silent as he was. A string of curse words from an open passenger window broke up the monotony even more and interrupted his scattered thoughts.

He had lost most of his compassion about a mile ago, most of his spirit within the last 500 yards, and most of the feeling in his face about two minutes ago. Without a watch, he had no idea how long he had been outside. Only that the wind and the rain were relentless, and the traffic was fearless. His shirt was soaked, his hair was drenched, water was leaking into his eyes, and the sound of the man cursing and calling him a bastard and a sonofabitch resonated in the deepest parts of his brain, and caused him to shiver and quake.

Johnny couldn't feel his hands, his shoulders slumped, his words were defeated and antagonistic, and his spirit was punched with filth and rage. The cars kept coming, his spirit kept shifting, and the sounds of the wind, the drunk, and the rain resonated in his brain. But he was determined to end his debts one way or another. He might have been a sonofabitch, or possibly even a bastard. And he might have been one step away from death, but he was determined to find peace.

The puddle splashed up around him. He muttered a few words under his breath, a prayer to the man upstairs. A few phrases cut through the darkness and offered the faintest hint of light. A vision of a blonde appeared before him with her hands crossed over her chest. The woman in black wore a top hat with long hair and a distorted face. The blonde opened her mouth, and a foul odor filled the air. One of burnt toast, broken eggs, and sour milk.

Her blue eyes lit up, her mouth opened wide—

similar to a black hole—and he was thrown back against the guardrail. Her arms stretched wide, and her lips were thin. The distance disappeared between them, and she pinned him to the metal with one hand and a bitter expression. He opened his mouth, but she waved it shut and spoke in a strange language that he didn't understand. Her pain was real, and so was his madness, and he had no idea which one would win in the end.

He stood taller and, with both hands, shoved her back. Words flew out of his mouth and held her at bay, as she lingered three feet from his face. He thought hard about that damn dog, shut his eyes to the insanity and the terrible choices he had made, and willed the strange spirit to disappear. When he opened his eyes, she was gone, and he staggered on.

ɔɛɔ

A red neon sign appeared up ahead, advertising free drinks and loose women. Women in black negligees with hair pulled away from their faces and sandy expressions met his gaze and smiled. With the last bills in his pocket, he decided a drink was in order.

Johnny stumbled up to the bar, plopped himself on an empty stool, and asked the woman behind the counter with the ribbon tucked in her raven hair to leave him the bottle. He tossed the remaining bills on the counter and turned his attention to the man with the acoustic guitar and the lava lamp standing next to him.

With his attention focused elsewhere, he didn't see the woman walk up next to him, nor did he see her sit down on the empty stool beside him. But he did recognize her voice.

"You're a fucking drunk," Gwendoline said.

His head whipped around, and her alabaster skin garnered his attention. "I haven't had a drink in *six* months."

"You're still a fucking drunk." She flicked the bar with her middle finger and swiveled on her stool. "Are you drunk now?"

He thought about the image that appeared to him in the wind and the damn dog all over again. "What does it matter?"

"It matters in every way you might imagine."

He looked past her and stared at a blank spot on a blank wall. "What are you doing here?"

Gwendoline waved her hand. "You first."

"Your smile doesn't get you as far as you think it will."

She flicked the bar again with the same finger. "I could say the same about your charm."

His gaze drifted around the half-empty bar, where the women wore tube tops and had ample cleavage, four flat-screen TVs were tuned to different stations, and two of the men had cowboy hats clamped down on their heads. His stool favored the left side over the right, and the bartender had a cell phone pressed to her right ear.

"You tried to leave me behind," Johnny said.

"Try a smile," she said, "and see how far that gets you."

He held the amber liquid up to his nose and sniffed. "Sober."

The drink plopped down on top of the bar untouched.

"You have suicidal tendencies," Gwendoline said.

He pointed in the direction of the door. "I think you need to step outside."

"If you run, do it with your head removed from your ass."

Johnny grimaced and took another look at the bartender. "You're a constant pain in my ass."

"You think?"

He nodded. "I know."

The damn thing was he needed that drink. He needed it more than oxygen. More than he craved a smile from a beautiful woman named Gwendoline. He tried a grin, and it got lost in the wind and died. The bastards were going to win, and all he had was a gun in one pocket and a bunch of bullets in the other. It was a fucking catastrophe.

A nightmare.

CHAPTER 11

The first bullet struck Johnny in the shoulder, and he spun away. The next bullet struck him in the bicep, and he dove over the bar, pulling Gwendoline with him. Mahogany and wood splintered around him. His mind shattered and gathered itself all over again. Chips spun in all directions, and a bullet blew a hole in the mirror above his head, leaving a trail of bold determination and broken glass in its wake.

His mind punched forward as his hands covered his ears, and the sound of men and women screaming ensued.

He poked his head above the bar, and a bullet whizzed near his left ear. He dropped back down, and, when Gwendoline opened her mouth, he clamped a hand over it. She glared at him and punched him in his wounded arm. He clamped his hand tighter, and she made a strange face, filled with anger and hatred.

He removed his hand from her mouth, popped back up, and fired his gun in the direction of the bullets. He heard one man go down, but there were two more left. When the gun clicked empty, he dropped the spent shells on the floor and loaded six more bullets in the chamber. His eyes drifted to the broken bottles and glass on either side of them.

The bartender must have given away Johnny's position with the cell phone call and the glance in his direction. It was Johnny's favorite bar in northeast Albuquerque, and he couldn't hide his lust for Hispanic women. Instead of opening up the world to conversation, the three men had entered the bar and put two bullets in him. Blood dribbled down his arm and mixed with the stained wood and the broken glass.

He had grabbed Gwendoline on instinct and yanked her over the bar with him. If not for the smoke and the muzzle flashes, the yelling and cursing, and a mess of tangled bodies huddling underneath the chipped tables, she might have uttered a never-ending string of curse words. In fact, he was a bit surprised she hadn't reverted to such tendencies. But Johnny was fairly certain that would come later if the two of them survived.

∽∾∽

Harrison had entered with two men much larger than himself, and he had already lost one man for his trouble. He hated Johnny fucking Chapman with every ounce of his being, and if it hadn't been for the informant bartender with the perky tits, he would have been forced to wait even longer to kill the sonofabitch. Harrison couldn't send a peasant to do the king's work, so he had been forced to come himself. If it was the last thing he ever did, he would shoot Johnny right between the legs and grin as the fucker bled out.

The plan was simple: blow Johnny away. He had enough firepower to kill off the Nazis, and he had one man left who could help him finish the job. Harrison had already lost three men for his trouble, but that was $150,000 he no longer owed. He had been chasing this asshole ever since that stupid mutt won the race he was supposed to lose, and Johnny had been indebted to him even before that.

Harrison didn't like to lose, and he didn't like being taken advantage of. Johnny had caused him to fail at both. And with another man down, he wanted to know when this shit was going to end.

While no civilians had been killed, Harrison wasn't opposed to sacrificing a few, especially the ones with the high-powered lungs, or the man to his right who was sucking his thumb. The chicken-shit bastard had already stained the front of his pants.

ᕫᕫᕫᕫ

The wall behind Johnny splintered and shattered. He had no idea how he had gotten himself into this situation—other than the stupid dog and phone call—and even more importantly, how he was going to get himself out again. If he didn't have Gwendoline beside him, he might have had an easier road ahead. But other than an ability to stare down men three times her size, she had no weapons at her disposal. Besides, even under better circumstances, she wouldn't have helped him, and she certainly wasn't going to help him now.

Anger etched her face, and the slap she had offered him was harder than he expected it to be. He had popped his head up twice now, and both times it had nearly been taken off. He still had a pocketful of bullets, but the two men had semiautomatic weapons and what appeared to be an unlimited supply of ammunition.

A sea of cars cloaked the parking lot, and the red neon sign offered the faintest hint of light. To help even the situation, he had shot out three of the overhead lights, but several more remained. A swarm of bodies had stumbled and staggered outside, but a half-dozen remained inside, including the man with the acoustic guitar and lava lamp, and the bartender hovering in the far corner.

His heart stuttered in his chest, the beats irregular and running on top of one another. His left hand shook at his side as his body worked off the excess adrenaline, and he used what was left of his mind to steady his nerves. Another slap from Gwendoline helped even out the situation. The air was filled with dust and smoke and the smell of fired weapons.

The wood on the other side of the bar was stained with blood, as it was behind. A thick haze encircled most of the area, and an ocean of anger filled the spot next to him. He turned his head away and coughed, as did Gwendoline. The desert was thick, and so was his mind, and still the haze lingered.

He had lost his watch when he had lost his cash: He hadn't bothered to replace the watch. Not that it would do him any good now. But it might help him capture the last moments of his existence.

The two men stayed on the opposite side of the bar. But he had no idea how long that would last.

℮⌃ↄ℮⌃ↄ

The man to Harrison's left had been shot in the chest, and he had bled out in less than three minutes. Harrison had watched the light leave his eyes, and it had filled him with a moment of sadness. It had been temporary and fleeting, but it had been there all the same. He had wasted more men than he had expected to on this mission to kill one idiot with a gambling and alcohol addiction.

If he had thought about it more, he would have waited until Johnny had downed the bottle of booze. But he had been anxious to end the charade, and he didn't think the little fuck had any fight left in him.

The woman should have slowed him down, but he nearly yanked her arm out of its socket as he pulled her across the bar, and, in Harrison's overanxious state, his bullets had slapped meaninglessly against glass and wood.

By the time Harrison had calmed, the slippery fuck was on the other side of the bar, and Harrison had been forced into a standoff with one man left. He had dropped his phone on the floor. Otherwise, he could have called in reinforcements.

And then there was another matter. He wanted to kill Johnny himself. Besides, Harrison had his pride to worry about, and he didn't want to admit to himself that he might have needed a bit more help. With the amount of blood already shed, he didn't want to compound the body count.

The pillar dug into his backside.

He had five more magazines in his pocket. He was fairly certain the man to his right had at least as many rounds, and Harrison had a six-inch serrated knife sheathed at his hip. He had worn a white cowboy hat for the occasion, and a belt buckle that was three times the normal size.

e/ɔe/ɔ

Johnny's legs wobbled beneath him as he attempted to crouch. A bullet zipped just above his head and lodged itself in the wood behind him. He took a tentative step to his left and then another and another, as he was still bent down nearly to the ground.

The gun was pointed at the ground, and Gwendoline slithered behind him. He stuck his hand above the bar and fired two shots for good measure in the general direction of his adversaries. Johnny was almost to the end of the bar, when a bullet skipped across the top and tossed woodchips in his face. He brushed the splinters aside and, with the wood, blood transferred to his hand. He wiped it off on his pants and felt a tentative arm around his waist. The arm was small and firm, as he continued to drag his body forward.

When he poked his head around the corner, a face appeared just off to his left. Before he could even think twice, Johnny fired. The man went down. Blood pooled from a wound in the middle of his chest. The strange man coughed and gurgled as blood dribbled down his chin. He covered the open wound with both hands, as more blood seeped between his fingers.

Harrison spoke for the first time. "You don't think you'll win, do you?"

Johnny squeezed the hand of the woman behind him

in reply. He fired at the direction of the voice and blew a chunk of concrete from the pillar. Two more shots and the chamber was empty. He inched back behind the bar, dropped the shells, and reloaded.

A chunk of the bar exploded just above his face. Gwendoline screamed, and Johnny's left hand shook.

A train whistled in the distance, or maybe that was just in his head. The sound erupted out of the darkness and filled his mind with images of the Old West. New Mexico. Albuquerque. His heart jammed in the back of his throat. He leaned too far forward, and a bullet caught him in the right shoulder. He didn't even blink, or cry out. He popped his head up and fired at a spot just a bit lower on the concrete pillar. Another chunk of debris exploded, and a deep voice uttered a string of curse words.

Darkness and quiet filled the dingy bar. And the train. And the sound of the rain slapping against the roof.

Johnny poked his head around the corner of the bar again, and four chunks of wood exploded in quick succession. He jerked his head back and closed his eyes, avoiding the worst of the splinters. One way or another, he was determined to end the madness.

Once again, the train whistle pierced the night air. His heart thundered in his chest. Blood spurted out of his three wounds, and he was gradually losing consciousness.

The voices told him to stop. To halt. He wasn't very good at listening to voices, or strange images that appeared out of thin air. He wasn't very good at stopping what he had already started. He wanted to finish this, one way or another. He was tired of the running, the games, the gambling, the debts, and the strange motels. And a woman named Gwendoline who had tossed him out on his ass two years ago.

"You really are a bastard," Harrison said.

Johnny didn't have any trouble recognizing the anger behind it. Gwendoline had a similar response when she shoved him outside and slammed the door.

Maybe his life would have been different if he had injected that dog, or maybe he was already headed down the wrong path before Gwendoline excluded him from her life.

And maybe sickness and persistence wasn't all it was cracked up to be.

Johnny squeezed her hand one final time, leaned over, and kissed her hard on the mouth. For a moment she let him, and then she turned her head away.

She touched the side of his face. "What the hell do you think you're doing?"

"Ending this."

She glared at him and punched him once more in his wounded shoulder. "You're fucking retarded. You don't have any idea what the hell you're doing."

Johnny kissed her once more for good measure. "Probably not."

He stood up and fired in the direction of the cowboy hat, and the little weasel fired a half second later.

Johnny Chapman struck the ground, but so did Harrison Barrymore.

∽∾∽

The next time Johnny opened his eyes, he was in a white, sterile room with a tube stuffed up his nose, and a needle shoved into the back of his hand. A woman who looked familiar was slumped in a padded chair with a magazine in her lap, and her long fingers turned the pages in a slow, methodical manner. The machine to his left beeped, and his head ached something fierce. Heels clicked on the tile floor of the hallway, and a woman in white drifted past.

"Where the hell am I?" Johnny asked.

Gwendoline's head popped up, and the magazine dropped to the floor. "You're awake—"

Johnny rubbed his head, and the needle in his hand moved with the rest of him. "You didn't think I was gonna make it?"

Gwendoline shook her head. "Well, you are the stupid bastard who got himself shot four times."

His whole body ached. "I was trying to save you."

"I don't need you to save me," she said. "I've never needed you to save me."

Johnny thought back to the bar, the woodchips, the broken glass, and the man who pissed his pants. "What happened to the other guy?"

She showed the faintest hint of a smile. "He didn't make it. But I'm glad you did."

He grinned for the first time in what felt like forever. "Yeah," he said. "Me too."

About the Author

Robert Downs aspired to be a writer before he realized how difficult the writing process was. Fortunately, he'd already fallen in love with the craft. Otherwise, his tales might never have seen print. Originally from West Virginia, he has lived in Virginia, Massachusetts, New Mexico, and now resides in California. When he's not writing, Downs can be found reading, reviewing, blogging, or smiling. To find out more about his latest projects, or to reach out to him on the Internet, visit the author's website: www.RobertDowns.net.

Made in the USA
San Bernardino, CA
14 February 2018